the Tree Keeper's Treasure

a novel

OTHER BOOKS BY TAMARA PASSEY

THE SHAFER FARM ROMANCE SERIES

The Christmas Tree Keeper

The Tree Keeper's Promise

HOLIDAY ROMANCE

Eleanor and the Christmas Carol Fudge

NON-FICTION

Mothering through the Whirlwind

the Tree Keeper's Treasure

a novel

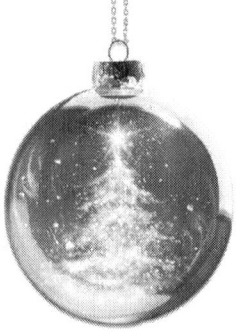

TAMARA PASSEY

Winter Street Press

The Tree Keeper's Treasure
Copyright © 2020 Tamara Passey
All Rights Reserved.

No portion of this work may be reproduced in print or electronically, other than brief excerpts for the purpose of reviews, without permission of the publisher.

This book is a work of fiction. All the characters, names, places, incidents, and dialogue in this novel are either products of the author's imagination or used fictitiously. Any resemblance to actual persons, places and events is coincidental.

Winter Street Press
winterstreetpress@gmail.com

Cover Design © 2020 by Sweetly Us Book Services | www.sweetlyuspress.com
Time lapse photo of lights by Pixabay and Photo of Snow Field Near Trees by Burak K. via www.pexels.com | Chains by www.brusheezy.com

Illustration by Edmund A. Smart III

ISBN-13: 978-1-7361384-0-3

1. Christmas–Fiction 2. Trees—Fiction 3. Miracles—Fiction

For Steve

PROLOGUE

William and Rebecca Shafer, Sutton Massachusetts, 1920

William held the dirt-covered shovel in one hand and wiped the sweat from his brow with the other. He filled the space in as he stood in the cabin doorway.

"Is it done?" she asked.

"Done and buried. Henry won't be bothering us again," he said.

Rebecca stopped her rocking chair. She held some fabric in her hand, her needle mid-stitch. "Are you sure it was the right thing to do?"

"The only way we'll have any peace around here is if that money is in the ground."

"Did you cover it like you said?"

"He'll never find it. You can take a look at it yourself tomorrow. Can't tell the soil was turned. I dug deep enough so I can make a root cellar for good measure. We'll be the only ones who know it's right under our feet."

Rebecca nodded. "Best go wash up for dinner. I can smell the underside of earth from here."

"Dinner? Looks like you're still sewing. What the devil is that thing anyway?"

"Mr. Shafer, don't use language like that around me," she teased. "I told you—a star for the top of our tree. It will match the quilt I made for the bottom of it. When I put them together, the points of the star will line up with the center of the skirt. See?"

"Only thing I see is that tree will be better dressed than our son," William said, chuckling as he left.

Rebecca returned to her embroidery, pushing the needle with gold thread up, then down. One stitch, two, then three. "There you go, little *x*."

She held the star at arm's length to admire her work.

"That ought to do."

CHAPTER 1

Tree Choosing Day, as Angela's daughter Caroline had named it, had already been rescheduled twice this year. Had they gone in September on Caroline's twelfth birthday, Angela would have been in her second trimester with this pregnancy, not her third. She would've been more agile, less round. But the pouring rain had kept them indoors that day. Another storm had raged the day they'd planned in October. "Storm" was putting it lightly. A category-four hurricane had bobbed up the coast. Though it was reduced to a category one by the time it made landfall in Providence, it had brought enough wind and rain to make their traditional tree-choosing event much too soggy.

Here they were, mid November, two weeks before opening weekend, and they hadn't found a tree. Not just any tree, but the one that would serve their family and so many of the tree-farm customers they welcomed each year. Of all the new family traditions she and Mark had started, Angela loved this one the most. It reminded her of their first trip to the Shafer Tree Farm and meeting Mark and Papa. That Christmas had changed their lives. Angela and her mother reconciled, Mark didn't sell the farm, and she and Mark found the hidden treasure—and each other.

She relished decorating the farmhouse for the holiday and opening weekend too. But this year, as exciting as it was to have a baby on the way, Angela felt like the holiday was approaching much faster than she could prepare for it. The closer it came, the harder it was for her to enjoy so many of the simple pleasures afforded by living on the farm.

"We have to go today," Caroline insisted. "Next week we'll be too busy getting ready."

"We could choose our tree the way the customers do, you know—closer to the actual holiday," Angela said lightly.

"Why would we wait? Besides, I know you don't like crowds that much."

Angela instinctively put her hand across her protruding belly. "Just not right now. I never knew how many people stare at a pregnant lady. And talk to them. And pat their stomachs," she said, her tone sharpening.

"Exactly," Caroline said. "Which is why we need to take advantage of the empty farm and choose our trees today."

"Trees? We only need one this year. Mark, tell her." Angela raised her eyebrows at Mark. He sat at the other end of the table, eating breakfast, with pretended unawareness.

"Tell her what?" He flashed a mischievous smile at Caroline. "She can choose as many trees as she likes."

"We only have room for one tree. This house has too much clutter as it is, and we aren't done converting the spare room for the baby," Angela said. Her hands landed forcefully on the table, and she sat up straighter.

Mark was behind Angela in one swift motion. Placing his hands on her shoulders, he kissed the top of her curly brown hair.

Angela relaxed. Married for almost three years, and she still melted at Mark's touch.

"I said she could *choose* as many trees as she likes, but you're right—we only need one for the house," Mark said.

Angela caught him still smiling at Caroline. "You two are conspiring against me. I can feel it." Not that she minded this—Mark struck the right balance when it came to being a stepdad for Caroline. He knew when to take sides and when to take a stand.

"Dorothy said I could choose a tree for their house." With that remark, her daughter left the table with her food half eaten and not so much as an "excuse me."

Angela sighed and reached for Mark's hand still resting on her shoulder. "Did you see that? She's only twelve. I thought I had a few more years before the eye-rolling started."

Mark took her hand and pulled her up into a quick embrace.

"She loves Tree Choosing Day," he said with a knowing smile.

Angela, Mark, and Caroline bundled up by the door, though Angela could only secure her coat's top buttons. She contemplated adding a scarf but offered it to Caroline instead. They planned to meet Papa and Dorothy on the trail after breakfast. Brett slipped in the side door like he did every morning, with a nod to Mark. Angela felt an odd rush of gratitude—not that it was odd to appreciate Mark's best employee, but it was strange to feel it so intensely.

This pregnancy had turned up the volume on all her feelings. What was generally a simple, happy reaction to someone showing up for work had become an urge to reach out and hug him for being there and helping Mark. Of course, she refrained. Brett may have worked there long enough to be considered part of the family, but no need to confuse the young man with a weepy good-morning hug from the boss's very pregnant wife.

"Good to see you, Brett," she said plainly, successfully disguising her excessive emotion.

"Hey, why don't you come with us?" Caroline asked.

Brett motioned to the counter and cash register situated near the side door to allow easy access for customers coming from the sales lot. "Someone needs to stay and take care of business."

Angela purposely looked around the empty room. "Yes, I can see you'll be beating back the crowds. C'mon, you're even dressed for it." She pointed to the hoodie and turtleneck he wore.

"She's right," Mark said. "We won't be missing any customers."

"But we'll be missing you if you don't come," Angela added.

"Okay. If you really want me along, I'll come. Let me finish with this mail." He simply moved a stack of envelopes and junk flyers from the front counter to the back and brushed his hands in the air. "There. Now I'm ready."

As they neared the seven-years' lot, the section of trees ready for the coming season, Papa and Dorothy stood waiting for them. Caroline ran ahead and hugged them both. Brett greeted them too. Angela appreciated that Mark didn't speed up but kept a steady pace next to her. Soon Papa and Mark exchanged a nod and a word while Dorothy put her arm around Angela's shoulders.

"Good to see you enjoying some fresh air. Are you getting your rest?"

"I think so. I should have at least another month before it's hard to sleep through the night." Angela replied, remembering the cumbersome heaviness of the last trimester.

Brett's question to Caroline caught her attention.

"Is it true you have a knack for picking out trees? What's your secret?"

Before Angela could stop her, Caroline answered. "No secret. The trees have an energy. Can't you feel it?"

Brett's face reddened, but he laughed it off. "How about I just watch what you do?"

"Suit yourself." Caroline straightened, walked closer to the line of trees on her right, and began explaining to Brett, "You see, some trees have this buzz about them. They're good for general miracles. Those aren't too hard to find with a little practice. But love matches are kind of, well, they're just . . . they're like a specialized miracle, and the tree gives you a kind of . . . I don't know, prickly feeling. In a good way."

Brett nodded, doing his best to listen attentively.

Angela glanced nervously at Mark.

"I had nothing to do with this," he said, palms up in mock defense.

Caroline paused and held up her hand for Brett to stop. "Here's a tree." She said it reverently as she stared intently at the branches. A moment later, she stretched out her arms as if she were about to embrace an old friend.

A bit of a chill ran along Angela's spine—unusual with all the extra body heat she was carrying these days. "Caroline, you don't have to be so dramatic."

"No drama, Mom. I'm respecting the energy," she said.

Angela, Mark, and Brett exchanged glances, and it appeared as though Brett was working hard to suppress a laugh.

Caroline stepped back and shot a pointed look at Brett. "Hope you felt that. That is some tree!"

She skipped ahead without any other explanation.

"What does that mean?" Brett slowed his steps and stared at the tree Caroline had been standing in front of.

Papa, who was bringing up the rear, passed Brett. "Means be careful what you wish for."

"I haven't wished for anything," Brett protested as he gave the drawstrings of his hoodie a tug and moved to catch up with the group. "Listen," he said to no one and everyone, "My dad is the one . . . well, he's the one waiting for . . . he's the one who needs a miracle."

Caroline called to him again. "Believe, Brett. That's how this works!"

At her daughter's words, Angela squeezed Mark's hand. Caroline's love for the trees was contagious.

Brett approached them, and Mark spoke first. "We're praying for your dad, Brett. Don't mind Caroline. She'd pick a love-match tree for everyone if she could."

"Caroline, are you sure you can't find a tree from one of the other two lots? We're getting farther away from the farmhouse, and only some of these six-years will be ready," Mark said.

"Yep. I have a feeling our tree is over this way." She gestured to her right.

Though she kept her eyes trained on where Caroline was headed, Angela could feel Mark's gaze on her. "I'm fine. Stop worrying about me."

"Not possible," Mark said.

"The air feels great, and this is good exercise," Angela insisted.

"When we get back, you're putting your feet up."

Angela shook her head. "We'll see."

Truthfully, she was feeling a little out of breath. Her lungs were unaccustomed to the extra occupant claiming more space by the day. She was having some sciatica pain and was light-headed, too, but she wasn't about to tell Mark. It was early in the morning, that was all.

Caroline was up ahead, as usual, stopping at one tree and then moving on to another. Brett walked a few paces behind Caroline and a few paces ahead of Mark and Angela. She thought of catching up to him to ask more about his dad but decided it was a question she could ask later. Papa and Dorothy followed a few steps behind.

"Don't mind us," Dorothy said. "We're taking our time today."

"We better catch up with Caroline," Papa said. "Looks like she's closing in on a tree."

As Papa and Dorothy moved ahead, Angela became instantly self-conscious. "Am I walking that slow?" she blurted out to Mark.

He shrugged. "It's not a race."

Dorothy turned around. "Don't you fret, Angela. No need to overdo." She must have also said something to Papa because Angela noticed his steps slowing.

As they all walked closer together, Papa announced, "That's right. We make adjustments for the little ones. They come along and change everything."

Caroline stopped at a tree. Fully stopped this time. Papa immediately stepped to her side to examine her choice.

Angela approached the Scotch pine they were gathered around, inhaling the sweet, sharp scent, Papa's words still lingering in her ears. Simple words and not hurtful in any way, but they struck at the heart of her fear. Namely, how this baby *would* change things—for starters, how she and Caroline got along.

When Angela was single, they'd survived more than a few hard times together and had always been close. But that had changed the day Caroline overheard Angela talking with Mark—behind what was supposed to be a closed door—and learned a baby was on the way, instead of Angela being able to tell her first. Caroline had been distant ever since.

Then there was Mark. He was holding her hand rather tightly and checking on her more frequently. For the last two-and-a-half years, they had a good balance of time together and time apart. Plenty of room for Angela's independent streak. She couldn't complain, or at least felt like she shouldn't. What wife wouldn't want her husband looking after her every comfort? What was so bad about his constant concern? It wasn't that she didn't appreciate this new protectiveness, she just didn't know what to do with it.

Angela bit her lip and pulled at a strand of her hair.

Yes, little ones came along and changed everything.

She watched Caroline walk beside the trees, happy but more intense than in previous years. How much she'd grown from the little eight-year-old girl when they first came to the tree farm into this confident, mature twelve-year-old.

"You okay?" Mark asked.

"Yes, but not if I have to keep convincing you of it." She grasped his hand, hoping to offset any harshness in her words.

"This one is a little tall, but I think it will be great for the farmhouse," Caroline said. "And this one right over here—for your house, Papa. What do you think?"

"You know your trees. Here, I brought the tags."

Caroline was already tying one of her hair ribbons around the branch. She'd grown three inches taller and easily reached an upper limb. As her daughter stepped back from the tree, Angela saw a melancholy smile cross her face. Angela moved closer and placed a hand on her shoulder.

"Nice tree. I like your choice," she said. "Are you okay?"

"Yeah, fine," Caroline said, but she shrugged away from Angela's touch.

Angela took a deep breath and released it slowly. Mark came up behind her, giving her shoulders a gentle rub. "Growing pains?" he asked.

"Maybe," Angela answered.

Mark moved to Papa's side, and their talk turned to soil conditions. Dorothy moved next to Angela and took an interest in Caroline's chosen tree.

"Don't fuss over Caroline. Tender age for her," she said in her matter-of-fact English accent.

"I thought she'd be happy about this baby," Angela said as quietly as she could.

"Don't talk like that," Dorothy said.

"Maybe she'd be happier if I were having a girl instead of a boy," Angela said.

"She'd be acting like this regardless. She's got to figure out how to handle all the changes in her life—and not only the ones coming when the baby is born. Speaking of handling changes, you realize you are going to have to slow down a bit?"

She may have asked it like a question, but make no mistake—this was Dorothy's way of making her point.

"I suppose," Angela said, none too thrilled.

Her attention was drawn to what Mark and Papa were talking about. Mark had a definite crease in his forehead. Papa stood with his feet firmly planted in one place, his arms across his chest, while Mark walked back and forth, gesturing.

"What could it be?" she heard her husband ask.

"That's for you to decide," Papa replied.

She stepped closer to Dorothy but kept an ear on Mark's conversation.

"I've never felt this from the trees." Mark seemed more exasperated now.

"Best be walking early every day until you figure it out," Papa said like he was pronouncing a verdict.

Both men took notice of Angela and Dorothy. Mark immediately maneuvered to Angela's side. "We need to get you back to the farmhouse to rest. Let's go."

They all turned back the way they came, but after a few steps, Angela stopped and looked about. "Where is Caroline?"

She searched the rows of trees to the north and south, but she couldn't see her daughter's curly hair or her pink-and-gray sweatshirt. The others scanned as they pivoted 360-degrees. There weren't too many places she could go. They were surrounded by acres of trees until a drop near an eastern ridge.

Mark shouted her name, and they waited. Angela heard a plane droning in the distance and a bird, probably a northern cardinal, calling nearby.

Caroline stepped out from the trees and into the path. "Guys, I'm right here."

"We're heading back," Mark said, taking Angela's hand.

Angela looked at Caroline, studying her face for clues, but Caroline didn't acknowledge her mother. Instead, she walked with Brett behind the rest of the group all the way back to the farmhouse.

Angela focused on her breathing as they walked, but the crease in Mark's brow distracted her. Finally, when she felt like she could walk and talk at the same time, she asked what was bothering him, careful the others wouldn't hear her.

"I wish I knew," he said with a distant look.

"Is it the trees?"

Mark nodded as he briefly met her eyes. He looked away but not before she saw confusion in his expression.

"Can you tell me?"

"There isn't much to say. This morning, when I walked the south lot, everything was fine. But when we reached the six-years and the trees Caroline chose, a cloud settled over me."

"What kind of cloud?" Angela asked.

"That's just it. I've never felt this way. I don't know what to call it. Maybe . . . dread?"

Angela's back straightened, and she gripped Mark's hand tighter.

"A cloud of dread. That's what I felt."

"Mark, that's awful. Is that why Papa suggested walking early every day?" Angela asked.

"Yeah, I'm the one who has to figure it out. Wait, you heard us?"

"Not on purpose . . . maybe a little." She raised her eyebrows to see if Mark's features would soften.

"I need to remember how loud Papa's voice can be." Mark shook his head.

Angela glanced over her shoulder to check on Caroline. Still there and walking contentedly next to the trees, while Papa and Dorothy were more centered on the path.

"Do you feel better now? I mean, it was just for a moment, right?"

Mark didn't say anything for another few yards.

"If anything, the feeling is getting stronger." Mark pulled at his neck with his free hand.

"Maybe you need to rest and put *your* feet up when we get back," she offered gently.

"Not sure if rest is going to fix whatever is wrong with the trees," Mark said.

Angela's stomach tightened. His declaration didn't help the tension she already felt over Caroline and this baby. Papa's words about babies returned, and tears stung her eyes. It didn't take much these days for emotion to overwhelm her.

Mark took notice.

"Sorry. Listen, I'll take care of the trees. No need for you to worry. That's my job."

"It's not just that," Angela said. "I hate the thought of Caroline feeling left out. I don't want to lose her." She put her hand to her eyes and squeezed them shut. "You heard what Papa said. Babies change everything."

With her eyes momentarily closed, she couldn't see how close Papa and Dorothy were. Without missing a beat, Papa chimed in. "Well, they sure do, but for the better. They change everything for the better!" He clapped Mark on the back as he said it.

Mark stopped and pulled Angela close. She didn't resist. Regardless of how tricky it was with her round, protruding belly between them, his hug slowed her racing heart and calmed her breathing.

Caroline breezed by them, darting to the farmhouse before everyone else. "I think someone is here," she called back to the group.

CHAPTER 2

As they approached, Angela could see a family in front of the farmhouse, and she quickened her pace. She eyed one of the porch chairs, feeling the need to sit after the long walk and brisk finish. Two small boys ran up and down the stairs and then the length of the porch, while a woman Angela guessed was their mother tried in vain to corral them. Caroline was already talking to a girl who stood an inch or two taller but appeared close in age.

Mark had taken long strides and was shaking the father's hand. Angela neared the base of the porch steps, and Mark turned to make room for her to stand next to him.

"This is my wife, Angela. I can't introduce you to our son yet, but as you can see, he's on the way," Mark said.

Angela smiled at Mark, loving how his soon-to-be fatherly pride came off him in waves.

"Congratulations," the man said.

"Thanks. Nice to meet you," Angela said.

"I'm Carl Shafer."

"Nice name!" Angela glanced at Mark, wondering about a possible connection. He'd never mentioned anyone named Carl.

"Thanks. That's my wife, Penny, the one chasing our boys." She waved from one end of the porch with her free hand, her other hand clutching one of the boy's shoulders.

Angela waved back as she climbed the porch steps and lowered herself into one of the chairs. "Do you mind if I sit?" she asked, though she didn't wait for an answer. Papa and Dorothy approached, and there was another round of introductions. Angela took some deep breaths, appreciating the immediate relief she felt. She spotted Caroline again, still talking to whom Angela assumed was the daughter in this family. She could see Caroline pointing and the other girl nodding. The sight of them laughing helped Angela relax even more.

Penny ushered her sons off the porch and toward their father. She asked Angela how far along she was and if this was her first baby. Angela asked about Penny's children and listened as Penny described her boys and how they kept her on the move all day.

"Macie is a big help," Penny said. "She's turning thirteen and has her teenage moments, but she's great with the boys."

Angela glanced at the girls again, taking comfort in this unexpected social visit.

Papa's voice carried a little louder than usual. "I thought so. Your great-grandpa's name was Carl too, wasn't it? You're the Manchester Shafers. My dad told us about your family."

"Is that right? We've heard a lot about the Sutton Shafers too. We ended up over this way and thought we'd come meet you for ourselves," Carl answered.

Angela couldn't hear the rest of what they said because Caroline came running over.

"Mom, can I show Macie the farm? The sales lot and maybe the south lot too? And the craft barn? Would that be okay?" Caroline asked, but she and Macie had already moved away.

"Sure, but don't be gone long." She glanced at Penny, not wanting to give the wrong impression. "You're welcome to stay as long as you'd like, but Caroline can lose track of time."

"We're in no rush. This was the plan for the day—to come and finally see the miracle Shafer trees," Penny answered, her gaze sweeping the farmhouse and sales lot. She leaned against the porch rail and sighed. "They sure are more beautiful in person than on the news."

Angela nodded as she searched Penny's expression. Something seemed off. She'd called them *miracle* trees and had that same wide-eyed wonder as some customers. Was she curious, or was it something more?

"Carl wanted to find out all about what makes them different."

"Oh." Angela worked to keep her voice even. "Papa is here. I'm sure he'll be happy to tell him all about the trees."

Not exactly a simple curiosity. Terrific.

Angela immediately pushed her suspicions aside. She was far too sensitive these days. After all, it sounded like they were extended family, and they weren't the first to be fascinated by the trees.

No need to overreact, she reminded herself.

"He's even heard you might have buried treasure here." Penny pushed her hair back over her shoulder. "I tell him he's going too far, but what do you think?"

The question startled Angela. She instinctively reached for her wedding band and spun it on her finger, her thoughts returning to the box and the soil and seeds. She sensed Penny staring at her.

"We found it." Angela said suddenly.

"A treasure? That's amazing. So, it was true?"

Angela could see the hunger in Penny's eyes for details. *And why not give her some,* she reasoned? *Better to put an end to the mystery before it grows out of control.*

"Yes. Christmas Day, four years ago. We found this." Angela held up her hand, showing off the diamond band.

"It's beautiful, stunning." Penny said. "And it was buried out there?" She motioned toward the trees and shook her head in disbelief.

Angela nodded. "That's probably a story for another day. Tell me how long you'll be in Sutton?" She deliberately changed the subject to something other than the trees and the box Mark's father buried. She listened to Penny but glanced at the group of men. Papa's arms were crossed over his chest, Carl had his hands in his pockets, and Brett was leaving the group. Mark rested his hand on the porch-step railing, but he wasn't smiling. His forehead still had that deep, concerned crease.

Mark gripped the porch rail and released it, then shifted his weight and scanned the parking lot. A breeze picked up and stirred through the trees. He focused on his cousin Carl as he talked about the tree farm his family ran in New Hampshire. As interested as he was in what Carl was saying, he couldn't stop himself from glancing at Angela. Seeing that she was resting on the porch, he felt some of the tension he felt on their walk subside.

But not all of it. The dread that had descended on him as they'd looked at Caroline's choice of trees had settled in his chest—like a cloud had moved from above his head and into his heart and lungs. The worst part was he didn't know why.

"It was time, that's all," Carl said.

Papa nodded solemnly.

"What was that? Sorry, I didn't catch the last part of what you said," Mark said.

"We sold the property last year. My brother-in-law hasn't been well. My wife is helping with their kids. We're looking to relocate to Sutton, where we can be close to them, at least for a few years."

"Sorry to hear about your brother-in-law. That's good of you to help," Mark said.

"It's my wife. She's amazing. There isn't anything she wouldn't do for her family," Carl said as he tipped his head in the direction of the women on the porch.

"Why don't you give Carl a tour?" Papa suggested.

"Hey, if you're busy, I understand," Carl replied.

"I'd be happy to. Let me check on Angela first."

Satisfied Angela was comfortable and getting to know Penny, Mark rejoined Papa and Carl at the base of the steps.

"Don't rightly know how to explain it. That's the funny thing about miracles," Papa was saying.

"Well, sure, but don't tell me you didn't exaggerate for the news reporter," Carl said in a teasing voice.

"Didn't have to. The trees are what they are—special to us and a lot of folks."

Mark wasn't sure how the conversation had turned to the news story, but he could guess.

"I'm ready," Mark said. "Come with me, Carl. We'll start near the craft barn."

Carl pointed to an area of the ground where the grading was visibly different. "What happened here?"

"Flood. Three years ago," Mark replied. "Damage to Donna's barn—the gift shop named for our family friend—could have been a lot worse if I hadn't added on to the house."

"Added on? How much square footage?"

Though he thought the question oddly specific, Mark supplied Carl with the dimensions.

"You boys go ahead without me. I'm going to stop here and help Dorothy," Papa said.

Mark watched him head through the barn door, then he and Carl continued over to the third-year lot of trees.

"That's great your grandpa still works on the farm with you. How old is he? Seventy-five?"

Mark had to think about it. "I guess he turns eighty-one this year."

"Man, that is the life," Carl said. "Working the land keeps you young. Have you thought about who you're going to have as a partner when he goes?"

Goes where? Is he implying what I think he's implying?

Sure, Grandpa was turning eighty-one, and it was obvious he couldn't work the farm forever, but who was Carl to bring it up like that? Mark finally responded. "Brett, my operations manager. He was here a minute ago . . ." Mark scanned the way they'd come. No sign of him. "That's like Brett. Always taking care of things. Couldn't ask for a better guy to be helping me. He's worked here since high school. It would be hard to find someone I trust more."

"Absolutely. Trust is a must," Carl said.

They continued walking on to the fourth-year lot, stopping at the first row, where Carl inspected a tree.

"Bark sure looks good. No peeling."

At the next tree, he asked, "What's this mesh? Wait, does that mean woodpecker trouble?"

"We've had some. The mesh is an experiment. It's working so far," Mark answered.

"I see the mulch you use. What about fertilizer?"

"Slow-release," Mark answered quickly. "About four pounds per hundred square feet in this lot."

"The ratio?" Carl pressed. "How much nitrogen, phosphorus, and—"

"And potassium?" Mark finished the question, growing impatient. "10-10-10."

"Nice. Needles keep their color. Gotta say, impressive."

Mark decided he had a few questions for Carl. He asked about the size of their farm in New Hampshire and about how it had recently sold.

Carl responded, but with few words.

"What is your dad doing now?" Mark asked.

"He's retired. He had these mini-strokes. My mom's a worrier, so they found a little place outside of Nashua. They're happy there. Seems like the farm is in good hands. It was hard for Penny and me to leave, but our brother-in-law hasn't been able to shake his cancer. Penny wanted to help her sister, so here we are."

Mark wanted to know what Carl was doing for work and where they were living, but Papa joined them.

"Hey, I found you," he said. "What did I miss?"

"A great tour," Carl said. "You know, you're coming into the busy season. If you need an extra hand or two, give us a call. We're no strangers to the work that needs to be done this time of year."

Papa rocked back on his heels and nodded. "That's a mighty nice offer. Hard to pass up someone who wouldn't need much training."

"We'll keep you in mind. Maybe we can compare notes. It's always nice to talk to someone who knows the business," Mark said.

After Carl left, Mark and Papa strolled through the empty sales lot. The tightness in Mark's chest was gone, but he still felt a trace of uncertainty.

"Any idea why this dread is getting worse? What is it with the trees on the western ridge?" Mark asked Papa.

"No clue. I'm four years from the connection I used to have. You know that."

"This feeling is so strong I thought maybe you would sense something too." Mark's voice trailed off. He thought of the year he'd become the keeper of the trees and the following year when he'd made the tree-keeper's promise. Papa had told him there was only one keeper at a time, so the fact that Papa hadn't felt the same thing wasn't a complete surprise.

"You've been saying you wanted clearer messages from the trees," Papa said. "Best be careful what you ask for 'round here."

"I know, but all I have is the feeling that something is wrong. Don't I need to do something?" Mark asked.

"At the right time. The trees will let you know."

Mark relied on Papa's conviction. With a baby on the way, he wanted to feel—no, he needed to *know*—the farm and the trees were safe.

"Remember, you take care of the trees, and they will take care of you," Papa said, perhaps sensing Mark's insecurity.

"What do you think about our new cousin?" Mark asked Papa, changing the subject as they continued their walk.

"Nice of him to stop over and introduce himself like that," Papa said.

"You think it was a friendly visit?"

Papa didn't answer right away, and they walked in unison a few more steps. "I'd say so. Young father and his family reaching out. Nothing wrong with that."

Mark couldn't argue with what Papa was saying, and yet he wondered if there was another reason for the man's visit and if it could have anything to do with the dread.

"'Course, not sure if he knows what happened between his great-granddaddy and yours," Papa said as if it were common knowledge.

Mark waited. "Do you want to clue me in?"

"The way I heard it, they didn't see eye to eye about a certain young lady. Instead of working the farm together, my great-grandfather stayed, and his brother—Carl's great-great-grandpa—stole his girl and went north."

"Wait, whose girl?"

"Exactly," Papa said.

Mark mulled it over. "It doesn't seem like he'd want to stir up trouble over a relationship gone bad this many years later."

Papa agreed with a nod.

"I mean, from the way you tell it, what would be the point? After all, his grandfather got the girl, right?"

Papa stopped walking as they neared the edge of the sales lot. Mark joined him, and they both faced the rows of third-year trees where they stretched to the horizon.

"Yep," Papa said slowly. "And *your* great-great-grandfather got all this."

CHAPTER 3

Tree Choosing Day had come to a close. Angela's feet had a throbbing new pulse, and her lower back had an aching pain to match. Her hips alternated between relaxed and sore throughout this pregnancy, depending on the day. Today they were sore. Rather than a dish of butter-pecan ice cream, all she craved was sinking into her bed. But she had one more stop to make—Caroline's room.

Angela found Caroline wide awake, wearing her pj's, and sitting cross-legged on top of her bed.

"Hey, you in there?" Angela motioned to her daughter's ears. "Happy with the trees you chose?"

Caroline pulled out her earbuds. "Totally," she said, still beaming.

"I'm going to bed. Don't stay up too late," Angela said, preparing to leave, but Caroline had more to say.

"Can you believe Mark's cousin has a daughter my age?"

"She seems nice," Angela said. She leaned over and gave Caroline a hug, but instead of saying good night, Caroline was ready to talk.

"Macie's great," Caroline said. "She says her brothers were cute as babies, but now they're big pains. She says it's been a zoo at their house ever since they learned to walk and talk."

Angela narrowed her eyes at her daughter.

"Don't worry, I know we don't say people are pains. Anyway, Macie and I both think turtles are cool and penguins are funny. Oh, and we agree pizza is a really weird food when you think about it. I mean, we eat it but they shouldn't call it a pizza pie. Pie should be reserved for apples or lemon meringue. She's calling me tomorrow. Do you think she can come over next week?"

Angela studied Caroline. Her daughter hadn't been this excited about a friend in a very long time. "That sounds fun. Did you already invite her?" Angela asked carefully.

"Sort of. I guess I suggested it. I don't know, we were talking about next week, and how school can be lame sometimes, and how friends you think are your friends turn out not to be, and how we both like the trees, and how walking around the farm together would be awesome. You know what I mean? Well, Macie knows what I mean."

Angela tried harder than usual to follow Caroline's twelve-year-old logic, hoping to discern if Macie was as interested as Caroline was in being friends. It sounded that way, and whatever their reasons for getting together, it meant that instead of trees, Caroline would have an actual person to talk to.

"I have so much I can tell her about the trees, like how people bring the trees to their homes and then the trees bring miracles to people's lives. And there's the special love matches—"

"Whoa, hold it right there. You don't need to explain all of that so soon. Remember what Papa taught you. Some people are more understanding than others, so be careful."

"She already knows the miracle part. She said her dad would talk about the news reports with the family at dinner."

"Is that so?" Angela sat down on the edge of the bed to rest her feet. She slowed her breathing and thought it through. If another tree farm were in the news, wouldn't Mark have done the same thing?

It's not that unusual, she told herself.

"Okay, then, choose a day next week, and we'll make it happen."

Caroline reached over for a hug. "Thanks. You're the best." She plopped onto her pillow.

Angela looked over her shoulder as she walked out of the room. "Good night, sweet Caroline."

She's happy, and I can get some sleep.

Angela retreated to her bedroom, where Mark was getting ready for bed. They'd remodeled the room the year they were married, but the week Angela found out she was expecting, she'd insisted on making more changes. She'd rearranged the furniture, put their bed against the east wall, and made space in the corner of the room for a rocking chair. Mark draped his shirt over it, but Angela swooped in to hang it up.

"Not a clothes rack," she said—nicely, of course.

"Right," Mark answered, pulling her into an embrace. "I think this baby is going to have the most prepared mother around."

"I don't know about that," Angela answered. "I still have to sort everything in the bottom kitchen cabinets."

"Babies don't crawl for, what, a year or two?" Mark said. Angela knew he was purposely exaggerating.

"Six months, which will feel like six days in our sleep-deprived state."

Angela searched for her pajamas—or the only clothes she could tolerate sleeping in. She'd resisted maternity pajamas on account of the circus-tent feeling. Did they think pregnant women wanted to sleep in pj's covered with elephants and zebras or, worse, clouds and storks?

"What did you think of our visitors today?" Mark asked.

Angela took note of his suspicious tone. "You mean your cousin?"

"Not exactly a first cousin," Mark answered quickly.

"Sounds like *you* think something about our visitors. Want to share?" Angela asked.

Mark started doing push-ups by the bed.

Angela made her way to the master bathroom to brush her teeth. She didn't like talking to him while he was doing push-ups. For one thing, she was sure he couldn't pay attention to her. If she were honest with herself, though, *she* would have a hard time staying focused on their conversation. Not her fault she found him attractive when he worked out.

She stood at the sink, brushing her teeth, remembering what Caroline had said about Macie and her dad. Should she tell Mark? But what was there to say—that they listened to the news? Any earlier concerns she may have had, she attributed to her hormonal oversensitivity. If Mark was already suspicious of them for some reason, her unfounded concerns wouldn't help.

She felt a twinge across her stomach, and she caressed her protruding belly as she finished brushing her teeth. Mark was on his last push-up.

"Papa told me about our great-great-grandparents. I guess Carl's great-great-grandfather stole my great-great grandfather's girlfriend. Even though he was supposed to inherit half the farm, they ran off to New Hampshire together. I don't even know if that has anything to do with me or Carl, but don't you think it's a little strange the way they showed up, wanted a tour, and offered to work here? I don't know what to make of it."

"I think they're a nice family, Mark. Wouldn't we do the same if we were in their position? I can't imagine what they're going through. Working on their family farm and his dad sells it? No wonder they're here offering to help."

"Well, I just get a weird feeling," Mark said.

"Yeah." Angela watched Mark as he reached for a towel. "You know what *doesn't* give me a weird feeling?" she said without revealing any emotion.

"What?" Mark asked, pausing.

Angela closed the gap between them and reached her arms up around his shoulders. He leaned in and kissed her. Once, twice, and, as usual, Angela was a little weak in the knees by the third kiss.

She pulled back. "Yeah, that." She smiled to herself, stepping away. "We better stop."

"Why is that?" Mark threw the towel on the bed and playfully reached for Angela. She cooperated, enjoying the way he wrapped his arms around her. She closed her eyes and breathed in the mixed scent of faint aftershave, the outdoors, and the salty heat of his neck.

"We won't get a good night's sleep if we don't," Angela said through more kisses.

"Is that a warning or a promise?" Mark asked.

"Oh—ow!" Angela said, her body tensing.

"What—what is it?" Mark asked.

"Ow. Wow, okay. Ow," was all she could answer.

"You're holding your stomach. Is the baby kicking?"

"If only." Angela caught her breath and looked at Mark with wide eyes. "I don't want to tell you what that felt like."

"What? You're scaring me here."

"A contraction, but it can't be. I'm only thirty-one weeks. Absolutely not."

"Right, too early for that, but why the pain?" Mark asked.

"I don't know. It's gone now."

"Here, you need to rest. You did all that walking today. Maybe it was too much."

Angela appreciated his concern but brushed it off. *He doesn't need to fuss over me*, she thought.

"It was only walking, Mark. Walking is not risky. It's good for pregnant wom—" This time, she bent slightly as she gripped her stomach. She no longer needed Mark's prodding to rest.

As she let her body relax into the mattress, her head on the pillow, she searched her memory for any similar experience when she was pregnant with Caroline. But that had been over twelve years ago, and this pregnancy was different in so many ways—morning sickness that lasted all day and double the fatigue. Her mother often reminded her she wasn't as young as she used to be. In all her memory, the only time she'd felt contractions with Caroline was when she'd gone into labor. The more she thought about it, the faster her heart pounded.

Perhaps she had overdone it. After a few slow breaths, her body relaxed. Mark was sitting on the end of the bed, watching her intently. He gently stroked her leg before resting his hand on her ankle.

She offered a smile. "It wasn't the walking. If anything, it was your kisses," she teased, waiting for the tension in his jaw to soften.

"You started it!" he said. "Wait, you don't think it was that, do you?" His expression shifted to alarm.

"Kidding. It's been a long day. I'm fine."

She lifted her head to fluff her pillow and emphatically put her head back onto it as if to prove her point. Mark reached over and kissed her forehead.

His lips no sooner left her forehead than another contraction seized her. She cradled her belly with one hand while she forced her eyes closed.

She would have said something to Mark, but it was like she'd been knocked breathless.

This is not good, she thought, *not good at all.*

Mark stood back. "That's it. I'm calling your doctor."

Angela opened her eyes. "I already know what she'll say."

She gingerly lifted herself from the bed, swung her feet to the floor, and cautiously stood.

"Why are you getting up?"

"She'll tell me to go get checked."

The hospital wasn't busy, and they were directed to maternity, where a nurse quickly escorted them to triage.

Angela attempted to answer her questions, but Mark kept answering first. She would have been annoyed under normal circumstances, but he sat next to her and rubbed her back in all the right places. Not too hard, not too soft.

They moved her to a room and connected her to a monitor, the nurse looking at Angela with one of those expressions—a controlled, give-nothing-away look that left Angela feeling like she was being studied.

"How do you feel now?" the nurse asked casually.

"Fine," Angela reported. No pain, but her heart beat a little faster at wondering what was going on.

"Good. We'll check on you in a bit—see if you're having any contractions."

"They've stopped, haven't they?"

"Looks that way." The nurse motioned toward the monitor. "And you're not dilated. Good news there."

"Then what am I? What was the pain?"

The nurse offered another restrained expression. This one felt like a how-could-you-not-know look.

"Likely Braxton Hicks."

Relief washed over Angela, then embarrassment, as if she'd been looking for her keys only to realize she'd been holding them in her hand.

Some four hours later, without a single contraction, and that was the verdict: false labor pains.

On the drive back to the farm, Angela vowed she would never do that again.

"The nurse said it was pretty common," Mark said, keeping his eyes on the road.

"For first-time moms! This isn't my first baby."

"But it's been awhile. Besides, she said you did the right

thing, coming in and getting checked. She said not to feel bad about it."

"Ugh. Don't they know when they say 'don't feel bad,' you immediately do?" She held her hands up in exasperation. "This will not happen again. I am due in January. This baby will probably need to be handing me the keys to the truck before I go to the hospital again."

Mark laughed. "Glad your sense of humor is back," he said.

"Go ahead. Think I'm kidding. You'll see. I'm not having this baby in December."

They made the last turn before the farm. The long road was darker than usual with no moonlight. A moment or two of silence passed before Mark asked, "Wait, why not? What's wrong with December?" Angela's last words had obviously sunk in.

"Like you don't know! A little thing called Christmas."

"Christmas is what's wrong with December?" Mark asked, confused.

Angela shifted, trying to move the weight of her stomach to the right side, taking pressure off her left leg and the sciatica nerve screaming at her. She leaned back in the seat, closed her eyes, and took a deep, calming breath. Without opening her eyes, she quietly answered, "I don't want to have this baby before Christmas. Caroline and I need one more together. She needs to have her mom all to herself for the holiday, one last time."

When she opened her eyes, she looked tentatively at Mark, searching for any sign of understanding, but there was not enough light to see his features. She felt tears begin to well up for no reason other than wanting this baby to arrive when he was supposed to.

She hoped the low light would obscure her face. No such luck.

"Hey, hey. Why the tears? Listen, it's going to be okay."

"You know I don't like it when people say that to me." Angela looked away more to deal with the tears than to avoid his loving gaze.

"Fine. Who knows if it will all be okay? Maybe it won't. This is a baby we're talking about. They have a mind of their own, I hear. So ready or not, they come when they come."

Angela chuckled and quickly wiped at her eyes. She turned to see Mark's I-mean-business face.

"That's better," she said.

Mark tossed one of his hands in the air. She reached for it and pulled it close.

"Thank you."

"What did I do?" Mark asked.

"You told me the truth," she said.

CHAPTER 4

Mark had planned to walk the trees early Sunday morning. With less than two weeks until Thanksgiving and their official opening weekend, he needed to get a jump on the day. Instead, he lay in bed, deep in thought. With his newfound cousin showing up at the farm, he had plenty to contemplate. But that wasn't why he was wide awake. The labor pains may have been false, but the hours at the hospital had been all too real. Rather than the far-off due date of January, the sense that this baby could come anytime—ready or not—had stayed with him. That, and watching Angela in even slight pain had left him feeling helpless.

Now, as she slept, he didn't want to take his eyes off her. Her forehead was relaxed, her expression content. He memorized the curve of her shoulder and how her long, slender arm stretched over to the edge of the bed as she rested on her side. He hoped she was having peaceful dreams. Not wanting to disturb the possibility, he slipped out noiselessly, and used the closet light to ensure he'd grabbed a clean pair of jeans for the day.

Mark chose to walk the six- and seven-year lots as he had with the group the day before. Not that he wanted to feel anymore dread, but if the feelings returned, maybe he could understand them better now that he was alone. The morning sky offered a pale-gray light, and the trees appeared motionless in the windless air. The lack of winter storms allowed them to get more work done, but the dry ground under his feet reminded him how much they needed snow to brighten the landscape. It would soften the lots' edges and transform a bleak line of trees into the winter wonderland visitors loved.

As Mark moved to the taller seven years, his chest felt heavy. He slowed his steps and moved closer to the trees. Unexpected images filled his mind, competing for airtime—one of him holding Angela's hand at the hospital the night before—and one of his parents hugging in the kitchen a few days before the fire. Mark had stumbled in on them. When they'd noticed, their eyes had lit up, and they'd motioned for him to join in their embrace. It was a simple but comforting memory. One image included Carl Shafer and his family standing near the farmhouse porch.

His stomach tightened, and he came to a stop, then took a few deep breaths and waited—for what, he wasn't sure. A different feeling or a new idea—anything to shed some light on what was going on or what he could do about it.

An image of the toolshed—the old root cellar where they kept the equipment in need of repair—came to mind.

That's strange, he thought. He turned and headed toward it. In his mind's eye, he could see the old flocking machine in the corner of the root cellar.

Maybe the old machine has a part for the new broken one.

He emerged from the shed without the part he'd hoped for, but one of the handles from the machine was in good condition and could be saved. He scratched the back of his head and looked around. He was trying to remember the image of the toolshed he'd had on the tree lot when he saw Brett waving at him in the distance.

"What brings you by this morning?" Mark asked.

"Good news. I wanted to tell you in person," Brett said, rubbing his ungloved hands together.

"I'll take it. What's going on?"

"My dad's insurance finally approved his hip replacement," Brett said energetically.

"That's great. He's been waiting a long time."

"Six months."

Mark could tell Brett was relieved for his dad, but for a moment, he wasn't sure why Brett had made an extra trip for the news.

Brett was already explaining. "He's scheduled for surgery next week."

"Wow, that's fast."

"I guess so, but he feels like he can't have it soon enough," Brett said. "The surgeon's schedule was full, but they fit him in. He's been in lots of pain, but you know my dad. He's semper fi, oohrah, and all that."

Mark had met Brett's dad a few times. He was a man of few words but had a generous smile if he liked you. And he was solidly built. Brett had cautioned Mark to never arm wrestle the man.

"Good—not that he's in pain but that his doctor can fit him in." Mark rubbed his chin and looked at the trees. Rain began to drizzle with a soft patter on the ground, and the air turned chilly. When Brett matched Mark's eyes, Mark understood why Brett had come in person.

"You're still the only one helping your dad?" Mark asked plainly.

"Yeah." Brett hung his head but brought it back up and kicked the ground. "My brother, he got married last year. He lives near Providence now, and they have a baby on the way."

Mark responded before Brett could ask.

"Take as much time as you need."

Brett's face registered relief. "You sure? I mean, I could come in one day a week."

"Don't even think about it."

"What about the farm?" Brett's voice faltered a bit.

Mark wasn't sure if it was emotion or the early morning air.

"Your dad needs you more than we do. You take as much time as you need." There was no question in Mark's mind. Brett needed to help his dad.

"I mean, can you hire a small army to take my place?"

There it was—Brett's classic humor.

"Don't worry. I will. In fact, that can be the job description for the ad: 'Can work like a small army—and eat like one too.'"

"I bring my lunch sometimes."

They walked back to the farmhouse in comfortable silence. Instead of going in the side door together, Brett paused before continuing toward the parking lot.

"You want a bite to eat?" Mark offered.

"I gotta get back. Thanks, though. Good luck with opening day," Brett said.

"Keep us posted about your dad."

"Will do."

Mark meant what he told Brett. He could take as much time as he needed. Brett was his dad's primary caregiver, and the recovery could take weeks. As good as Mark felt about insisting Brett take time off, that would leave them shorthanded. They may have joked about a small army, but it was truer than Mark wanted to admit. He would need helping hands, a lot of them.

Carl Shafer. The name forcefully came to Mark's mind, though accompanied by a fair amount of resistance. He was an obvious solution and had already offered his help. That had fueled Mark's suspicion even more.

Mark huffed as he moved a large log to the left of the side door. They'd planned to build a bench out of it, but he wasn't going to get to that project anytime soon.

Why is Carl so eager?

Mark's conflicted feelings weren't evidence of anything untoward, and ruminating about them wasn't going to help him get any work done. All he could do was reach out to Carl and hope for the best.

※

Mark ended the call, set his phone down, and pushed back from the desk. There was one more temporary worker he knew he could call, but he was twice Brett's age, and though Mark hated to admit it, he didn't have Brett's stamina. Then again, did anyone? And more importantly, did Mark have a choice? He needed help. He grabbed the phone and dialed Stan's number.

"Stan, what would you say to some full-time work for a few extra weeks this year?" Mark listened as Stan rambled on about his knee injury, some trip he took with an old army buddy, and his step-daughter's wedding.

"But, hey, you've always been good to me, Mark. I want to be there for you," Stan said as he wrapped up his year in review. "I'll have to watch my knee, but you can count on me."

Mark hesitated, wishing he hadn't called. "Great. So how about Thursday of this week?"

"That soon?" Stan backtracked. "I've got jury duty, and I promised my brother I'd help him rebuild the engine in his work truck. I can start a day or two before Thanksgiving."

It wasn't much different than when he would typically come in to help.

"Okay, that's good of you, Stan. See you then," Mark replied. As he ended the call, Papa came into the room. Mark tried to disguise his frustration—a useless effort around Papa.

"Who was that?" Papa asked.

"Stan," Mark said.

"It's not even opening weekend and you're calling him?"

"Brett's dad is having surgery," Mark stated. "I wouldn't say I'm desperate yet, but I will be if I can't find some extra hands."

Mark stood and cleared things from his desk, hoping to distract Papa and maybe change the subject.

Papa put his hand on the back of the chair opposite the desk. "What did Carl say?"

Mark tensed. "I haven't asked him."

"Seems he'd be your first choice. Taking the hard road?" Papa tilted his head as if he were sorting out a puzzle.

"Maybe." Mark strode to the window on the other side of the office. He stared in one direction and then the other, his hand gripping the back of his neck. "I'm not sure about him yet."

CHAPTER 5

Angela woke to Caroline knocking on her door. Unclear of the day or time, she sat up slowly. "Come in," she called. Caroline bounded into the room and onto the end of the bed.

"Mark said he didn't want to wake you, but you must be starving. Gotta feed baby. Want some breakfast? I made waffles."

"You cooked?" Angela asked. Her stomach responded with a growl, and a smile found its way to her face.

"They might not be as good as yours, but like you say, the syrup will save them."

"Thanks, honey. I'll be out in a few minutes."

Caroline left the room as quickly as she came, calling behind her, "Don't take too long, or they'll get cold."

Angela shook her head at the role reversal. Twelve was a little young to be mothering her mom, but that was Caroline—taking charge and looking out for the both of them.

She eased into the only clothes that would fit at thirty-one weeks, soon to be thirty-two. The soreness in her muscles from the hospital chairs and bed made every moment a slow struggle. She cringed. Early labor, false labor—the whole night had been a disaster.

The smell of waffles reached her, and she moved instinctively to the kitchen.

"Mom, are you coming?" Caroline was already piling a plate full for her.

"I'm here," Angela said. "You didn't tell me you cooked bacon, too."

Now her mouth watered as she added butter and syrup to the feast on her plate. How had she gone from hungry to ravenous on the short walk from the bedroom to the kitchen?

She took a bite, then a second. The doorbell rang, and she and Caroline looked at each other.

"I'll get it," Caroline said as she jumped up from the table.

Angela reluctantly set her fork down. This visitor would need to have a good reason to be interrupting her still-warm breakfast.

"Hi, Grandma!" Angela heard Caroline say, unable to see the front door from where she sat at the end of the dining-room table.

"Good morning!" Her mother's singsong voice rang through the farmhouse. "A little late for breakfast, but at least it smells wonderful."

"It *was* a good morning," Angela mumbled to herself.

"What was that? Do speak up, dear." Cathy stopped short of the table where Angela was sitting. "My, you look tired."

"I made waffles and bacon, Grandma. Would you like some?" Caroline asked.

Angela inhaled sharply at Caroline's announcement. She appreciated the breakfast, and Caroline hadn't done anything wrong, but she could feel her mother's increasing scrutiny of the situation.

"Darling, how sweet of you. I ate breakfast two hours ago and don't want to spoil my lunch. I also don't have very much time. I'm meeting Gary in town. But thank you."

Angela gobbled up the rest of her waffle as she carefully watched her mother. She seemed happy enough with Caroline, but why was she here?

"Angela, I must say, I haven't seen you like this before. I wasn't expecting you to look—"

"Just say it mother," Angela said dryly.

"Ghastly."

Angela might have had more patience for her mother if not for the hospital claiming all of it the night before. She pushed the plate away and stood up from her chair. She looked directly at Caroline, thanked her for breakfast, and then locked eyes with her mother in a cold stare.

"Excuse me. I have work to do," she said.

"What on earth has taken hold of you? I simply stopped by to say hello."

"Actually, you said I look ghastly. And you never just say hello. You always have reasons. What is it today?"

Her mother fumbled with the keys in her hand before putting them in her purse.

"I've spoken with Dorothy. I'm meeting her at Donna's barn. I'm searching for a few more items for the charity auction. I thought she might have told you I was coming. I see she probably didn't have the chance if you've barely fallen out of bed."

Waffles, bacon, and a side of judgment was not the best way to start her day. She rearranged the robe she'd thrown on and chose her words carefully.

"If you'd spent five hours in the hospital last night, you'd take a late breakfast too. Why am I standing in my own house defending myself to you? Aren't you the one person who should have at least an ounce of compassion for her pregnant daughter?" Angela was sure her blood pressure was rising. She could feel her heart pounding and hands curling into fists. With the doctor's words about getting rest still ringing in her ears, she grabbed the glass of juice on the table and drank it down.

Cathy sat down at the table, allowing her purse to slide off her arm and onto the floor. She looked back and forth between Angela and Caroline.

"I had no idea. No one told me. Are you okay? Is the baby okay? Should you be lying down?"

"I'm fine," Angela said.

"Why were you in the hospital? Who drove you? Why didn't Mark call me? What about Caroline?" Her voice rose in pitch with each question.

"I told you, I'm fine. Dorothy came to the house." Angela set her glass down. She could see her mother's injured expression. "She's much closer than Providence."

"Of course," Cathy said.

Angela regained composure. "Caroline, can you clear the table?"

"Sure," she answered. "You and Grandma probably need to have one of your talks."

That brought a smirk to Angela's face. "Mom, look, it was a false alarm. I wasn't in labor. Believe me, if they'd kept me or if it was anything more serious, we would have called. Okay?"

Cathy pulled a handkerchief from her purse, her hands shaking as she dabbed at her forehead.

"I will bring Caroline home with me for the weekend. You'll have a quieter house, and you can get some rest," she said, returning to a lower tone.

Angela squared her shoulders. "She's the one who made me breakfast today. She's twelve now, and I need her more than ever. You're not taking her anywhere."

They stared at each other, and a dish clanged in the kitchen.

"Fine. I'm calling the service. They can have someone here in one or two days. Laundry, cooking, cleaning—they'll do whatever you need them to." Her mother lifted her chin, satisfied with herself.

"Mom, seriously? They were Braxton Hicks. You're overreacting." Angela's eyes widened at her mother's over-the-top offer, though she did consider it for a minute before she came to her senses. "No way. Having someone here would get on my nerves."

Her mother forced a breath. "Where did I go wrong?"

"It's not necessary."

"It's such a simple solution," Cathy continued. "It's no trouble for me. This place may be rustic, but there's no reason you can't have helping hands.

"It's a no. Not gonna happen," Angela insisted.

"But you are carrying my grandchild. I've got to do something to help."

The pleading in her mother's eyes swayed Angela. "If you want to take Caroline shopping with you, she'd probably like the break. But as for helping me? Let's have fewer stressful conversations like this one. Deal?"

Her mother nodded as she dabbed at the corners of her eyes again. "Yes. Agreed. Or however you say it. Deal."

Her mother stood, and though they had found some kind of middle ground, Angela did not feel the need for a hug. Cathy seemed bewildered, as if she didn't even know how she got to the farmhouse in the first place.

"Maybe Dorothy is waiting for you. I'll let Caroline know to be ready when you leave. Are you sure Gary won't mind?"

"Not at all," her mother insisted.

Caroline was thrilled to have an outing with her grandmother, and though Angela couldn't match her level of excitement, she did feel like it was a happy compromise. Caroline could have some time with her grandmother but not be gone the entire weekend. No reason to add to the distance between them already.

※

Angela did have to admit, with a quiet house she could get a few things done. She could pay some bills, do a few loads of laundry, and get started on the closet in the baby's room. As she walked from the kitchen to the master bedroom, she caught a glimpse of herself in the mirror. Her hair was about as matted and greasy as she'd ever seen it, and she was wearing one of her old maternity T-shirts—so ratty she had relegated it to sleepwear. She didn't even remember putting it on when she got back from the hospital in the early morning hours. She let out a laugh. No wonder her mother had said she looked ghastly. Too bad she hadn't seen herself before her mother had arrived—she might have agreed with her instead of taking offense.

She knew she needed a shower, but even the thought made her tired. Maybe what she needed was a nap!

Sleep in, eat breakfast, take a nap—that's a great routine, she thought. *A few more days of this, and I will need one of Mother's employees.*

She eyed the basket of laundry in her closet. She didn't mind the chore, but the washer and dryer were in the basement. That meant climbing the stairs. She sighed and resolved to recruit Caroline's help when she returned from shopping with Cathy.

She sat in the rocking chair in her bedroom, closed her eyes, and thought through what absolutely needed to get done. Even while sitting, she felt weary. There was tired, and then there was pregnancy tired. One version she could push through and force herself to keep moving. She was no match for the other. Yes. Instead of working, she needed to take advantage of the quiet house for some productive rest.

But before she could make her way to the unmade bed, she heard Dorothy call from the front room.

"Where is my darling Angela?"

She immediately pulled her hair into a ponytail. As quick as she could, she cast off her robe and grabbed one of her newer maternity shirts, replacing the old one.

"In here," she called to Dorothy. "I'll be out in a minute."

When she arrived in the front room, Dorothy was making a cup of tea in the kitchen.

"Would you like one, dear?" she asked. "I know you had quite the night."

Angela declined. "I'm full at the moment. Caroline took good care of me with some waffles."

"It smells like bacon too," Dorothy said. "Come sit down. I had a little visit with your mother."

Angela joined Dorothy at the table but cringed at the image of Dorothy visiting with her mom.

"My mother was in one of her moods this morning. She took one look at me and called me ghastly. Did she mention that?" Angela asked.

"Tut-tut," Dorothy said. "I'm on your side, child. Your mother didn't stay long. She cruised the barn looking for specialty items for her charity auction. She said she couldn't see anything 'unique' enough."

"See, what did I tell you?"

"She was just anxious to go, I think. Whatever your conversation was, it left her unsettled."

"You're being generous. I'm sorry if she was rude," Angela said.

"No, not rude. Preoccupied. She's worried you might be overdoing it."

"I slept in, that's all." Angela stood. "I'm sorry, Dorothy—"

"No apologies, dear. Take it from me, there's nothing that tugs at the heart of a mother like seeing her pregnant daughter in the last trimester. Even the most carefree mothers can get a little bit . . . overprotective."

"Unsettled, preoccupied, overprotective? You give her the benefit of the doubt every time, don't you? She wanted to call her service! Can you imagine me having some sort of butler or maid around here? Ridiculous! It's like she doesn't know her own daughter." Angela walked over to the sink and loaded dishes into the dishwasher.

Angela noticed that Dorothy was sipping her drink and avoiding eye contact, though there was a slight smile at the corners of her lips.

"You don't think it's ridiculous?" she dared ask.

"I can understand how it would make you uneasy. But keep in mind it's your mother's style. It's her way of showing love." Dorothy set the cup down and let out a little sigh. "I don't think you need a house full of servants waiting on you hand and foot, but it doesn't hurt to slow down a bit. Don't be tempted by all the things you could do. Heaven knows a tree farm never runs out of work to be done. Please take care of yourself and that little one. If you need something done, call me. That's why I'm here. I told you we're taking a shorter trip to Oregon this year and I'll be back to help you during the last few weeks."

Dorothy's words brought tears to Angela's eyes. The softness in her voice and the loving way she could interpret her mother's actions humbled Angela. Her cheeks heated with regret at the way she had spoken to her mother. Why was it so clear now but not moments ago?

Dorothy's understanding nature and reasonable offer for help was so much more comforting. She thanked her and promised she would call if she needed her.

After Dorothy left, Angela returned to her bedroom, and this time she managed to crawl under the covers and rest her head on the pillow. How good it felt to settle down and let the weight of her body sink into the bed. She pulled the blanket around her shoulders against the chill in the air.

So what if I need a nap after sleeping in? she reasoned. She was still getting comfortable when the doorbell rang. She rolled to her back and stared at the ceiling. *No such thing as a quiet house!*

Angela didn't even bother to fluff her hair or change her clothes. She opened the door, and there stood Penny Shafer with her two young boys and Macie. A pleasant surprise to be sure, but Angela immediately regretted sending Caroline with her grandmother.

"How nice to see you, Penny. What brings you by?" she asked.

"We planned to visit the farmer's market today. I baked some bread this morning and thought I'd bring you a fresh loaf. You don't have a gluten sensitivity, do you?"

"Thank goodness, no," Angela said as she accepted the gift. "This is thoughtful. You didn't have to go out of your way."

"It was on our way, and I wanted to say it was great to meet you yesterday."

"Would you like to come in?" Angela asked. She looked at the two boys squirming at their mother's side and wondered if her home were childproof.

Penny smiled. "We'd love to, though we can't stay long."

"Is Caroline home?" Macie asked.

"I'm sorry. She's in town with her grandmother," Angela answered.

Penny looked as disappointed as Macie did. "Why don't we visit on your porch? We don't want to intrude."

"Let me grab my coat," Angela said. She put the bread on the table, and when she returned, Macie had taken the boys for a walk.

"I'm sorry Caroline isn't here. I know she would have loved to visit with your daughter."

"I should have called ahead. You had no way of knowing we would stop by."

"Please, let's get them together again soon. It seems like they get along great, and I'm happy for Caroline to have a friend."

"I feel the same way about Macie. She helps with her younger brothers all the time and misses the friends she had in New Hampshire."

"Are you planning to move here to Massachusetts? Or is it more like window-shopping?" Angela asked.

"If we can find something affordable, we hope to be settled by the holiday. I'm helping my sister with her kids. Now that Carl's father is officially retired, Carl can figure out what he wants to do. Sure, he could find work at another farm in New Hampshire, but it's a little too close, if you know what I mean."

Angela was beginning to get the picture. If Mark sold the farm, she could not imagine him going to work for any of the surrounding farms in the area. There was a great friendliness among the neighboring tree farmers, but working for a competitor would be awkward at best.

They covered a few more topics, like schools in Sutton and some of the surrounding towns. When Angela shifted uncomfortably, their conversation changed to her pregnancy. Angela had nothing to lose by asking Penny if she had ever had false labor. Soon they were talking as though they'd known each other for years, sharing pregnancy woes and delivery stories.

When Macie returned with her brothers, Angela felt a twinge of sadness that they would be going.

"Please come back anytime. Here's my number. We could even have you to Sunday dinner," Angela implored.

"I doubt Mark would want you hosting anytime soon. We could come after dinner, or, better yet, we could bring it," Penny said.

"That's not necessary. Your company is the gift."

After Penny and her children left, Angela sat on the porch, basking in the low afternoon sun. She hadn't accomplished anything today. Not the bills, not the laundry. She hadn't even looked at the closet in the baby's room. She pushed her hands deeper into her coat pockets, pulled her shoulders tight, and released a long sigh. She wasn't in the hospital, she had family and friends looking out for her, and she only had to wait two short months to hold her new baby.

No need to stress.

CHAPTER 6

Mark made the last call to the restaurant manager. Everything was ready for Saturday night. He was taking a chance to plan a date for their anniversary almost a month early, but he was counting on two things to land in his favor: First, Angela would be surprised. Second, it would be evident he'd remembered their anniversary and planned something without her prodding.

There was a new steakhouse in Sutton that had several private party rooms. The manager was happy to accommodate Mark's request for tropical-themed food and decorations. He didn't care about the cost, so long as when Angela entered the room, she didn't think of winter or Christmas. It's not that they had any strong desire to vacation on some island, but more than once, Angela had told Mark that their anniversary celebrations didn't need to be holiday-themed just because they were married so close to Christmas. Of course, people in the tropics celebrated the holidays. Still, as long as he and Angela were in New England, the Hawaiian Luau Chicken and Aloha Paradise Cheesecake would give them a break from turkey and stuffing.

All he had to do was to figure out when to tell Angela. If he told her too soon, she'd ask questions and ruin the surprise. But if he waited too long, she'd protest a dressy date night without any notice.

When he stopped by the house to change out of the extra morning layers he was wearing, Angela decided for him.

"Can you believe our anniversary is next month?" Angela asked.

Mark wasn't fooled. He knew a test when he heard one.

"Huh, that can't be right," he said flatly, keeping his face as impassive as possible.

He could feel her eyes studying him, but he didn't flinch. Instead, he stayed absurdly interested in the clothes in his closet.

"Well, it is. Only six weeks—five and a half, really. It's only going to get busier around here," she said.

There it was. She was worried Mark would either forget or become too busy. He couldn't help himself. He pushed it a little further.

"Six weeks. We've got plenty of time." He shrugged and briefly checked her reaction. Alarm flashed in her eyes.

"Um, remember, we promised we wouldn't let our anniversary get lost in the holiday rush?" Angela said, her voice rising.

"Hmm, can't say that I do," Mark shot back as he pulled a shirt over his head, helping to conceal his humor.

Angela's mouth hung open, and she snapped it shut. "Mark," she started.

He gave her a flirty, half-grin as he ran his belt through his pant loops and buckled it. She watched from the doorway. He crossed the room and pulled her in for a hug while keeping his eyes trained on hers.

"What are you doing?" she asked.

"Saturday night. Do you have something dressy?"

He watched the battle of emotions on her face—the surprise in her eyebrows, the suspicion on her lips.

"We have plans?" she asked. "*You* made plans?"

He sported his most flirtatious smile.

"But when? Before I said anything?"

"It would seem so," he said smugly.

※

Monday proved to be a long day. Mark made his way to the office at the farmhouse. He checked his messages and confirmed that of all the people he'd called, there were only two who could come in part-time, and that wasn't until after Thanksgiving. He needed full-time help to prepare for opening weekend. He even considered calling Brett and asking him to come in for a day, but he quickly shook off the thought.

Angela softly knocked on the half-open office door.

"Hey, there you are. Are you hungry for dinner?"

"Yeah, I'm wrapping things up right now."

"Looks like something's bothering you. What's going on?" she asked.

She knew him well.

"It's tough finding someone to replace Brett, that's all." He ran his hands through his hair and sat back in his chair.

"Why don't you call Carl?" Angela asked.

Mark sighed. "I don't think I trust him."

"Have you known him long enough to have a reason not to?"

"You said dinner was ready?"

"You're avoiding the question."

Mark searched his desk for nothing in particular, then looked at Angela. "That's just it. I haven't known him long enough to have a reason *to* trust him. What I do know is that he asked Papa about the miracle-tree news story. I don't know what else he knows. If there is one kind of man I don't want roaming around my farm, it's a treasure hunter."

"He has a family, and he's looking for a job. He seems pretty down-to-earth to me."

Mark stood, anxious to end this conversation peacefully.

"Those same two things could make him desperate too. Forgive me if I'm not his biggest fan. Maybe you want to see the good in him because Caroline and Macie are getting along. Come to think of it, you and Penny are too. Maybe you're just seeing what you want to see."

Mark regretted his words. Angela was blinking back tears. This was not like her at all, and even though he was sure her pregnancy was the culprit, he was still having a tough time remembering to be more sensitive.

"Hey, I didn't mean it like that," Mark backtracked.

"I'm fine," she said, taking a deep breath. "I think you should give him a chance. That's all."

She appeared to regain her composure.

"Dinner is waiting," she said before she left.

Mark got an early start Tuesday morning. He stacked an extra pile of wood, made himself a breakfast sandwich, and even threw a load of jeans into the washer. Farm work and food were necessities, but usually, when Mark started a load of laundry, it meant he was procrastinating something. Today that something was picking up the phone and calling his newfound cousin, Carl.

Angela had encouraged him to, and though she'd been sincere, he hadn't responded well. He'd practically accused her of bias and brought tears to her eyes.

Maybe he'd put off calling Carl long enough, but he was still bothered by some unanswered questions. The most obvious one—why had they sold their farm in New Hampshire? Had it failed because of something like crop devastation or was it due to bad management? It was hard to ask someone if they were a lousy business manager. He also wanted to know why now. Why had Carl shown up at the same time Brett happened to be taking a leave of absence? How could it be Divine Providence at work and also raise his suspicions? Why those two feelings were so closely related, he didn't know. Perhaps there was only one way to find out.

He switched the load of jeans from the washing machine to the dryer and retreated to the back office to make the call in private.

"Carl? Mark here. Is this a good time? Got a question for you."

Mark explained how one of his best employees needed some time off for family matters. He said he didn't need to tell Carl how crucial the upcoming weeks were, not to mention how busy it would get after opening day. He took a deep breath and asked Carl if he meant what he said the other day about being available.

"I'd love to help in any way I can," Carl said enthusiastically.

"Are you free to start soon? Full-time?"

"I can start tomorrow, or even today. I can be there in two hours."

Even though Mark needed help, he didn't expect Carl to be available so soon. Hearing the enthusiasm in his voice only increased Mark's suspicion. Why was he so eager? Angela would say it was because he was out of work and glad to have a job. What was Mark's problem? Didn't he want him to start as soon as possible? Yes, in theory. Maybe he'd expected Carl to need some time, and that would give Mark some time—to get over himself, apparently.

"Do you need to talk it over with Penny? Have you found a place to live around here?" Mark countered.

For the first time in their conversation, there was a pause. Maybe Mark had asked too much. Did it sound like he was prying?

"We're still looking. Penny is trying to find the best school for the kids," Carl finally replied.

"Oh, sure," Mark said, though he worried he'd asked too much.

"Tell you what. I will talk to Penny and get back to you," Carl said.

"That's fine. No problem. I'll look forward to hearing from you."

The clothes in the dryer were done and needed folding, and, as was often the case, now that Mark wasn't putting something off—his desire to do laundry vanished. Not only that, but he had plenty of farm work waiting for him. He knew better than to start a load of laundry and not finish it, though. He didn't mind pulling his clean clothes from the dryer every day, but Angela wouldn't stand for it. Especially not now that her cleaning and organizing efforts had started to overflow out of the baby's room and into every corner of the house.

Mark folded his jeans as quickly as he could, wondering why he hadn't just accepted Carl's offer. If he didn't hear from him soon, he would set aside his suspicions once and for all and call him back.

CHAPTER 7

Angela smiled every time she thought of Mark planning something for the two of them. Saturday was finally here. He'd almost fooled her, acting indifferently about their anniversary, only to surprise her by having a plan. Though she had no better idea about what that plan was other than to wear something dressy, she loved the anticipation she felt. Shopping for maternity *anything* wasn't so fun at thirty-two weeks, but she'd found a black dress that had a sweetheart neckline, landed at her knee, and allowed plenty of room for baby.

Mark had gone into town to find a part for the flocking machine, and Caroline was staying with her grandmother—something Mark had arranged. Cathy would bring her home Sunday night. That meant Angela had the house to herself. Today was the day to tackle the baby's room, which had formerly been Mark's sister's childhood room. At Angela's request, Mark had already repainted it and replaced the old shag carpet with new wood floors. The closet was the last holdout—full of old winter clothes, a broken vacuum, and old boxes full of office papers. Not her favorite thing to do, but Angela felt as if cleaning out the closet was the only thing that mattered, as if the world could not keep turning until the closet was cleared and full of things only the baby would need.

Music played from the studio, the one Mark had built for her before they married. It was long past lunchtime, and she was craving roast beef again, something she wanted no matter how much she seemed to eat. She wasn't sure if cravings went on for days or if it was just easier to keep eating the same foods. All her creative energy was devoted to cleaning the farmhouse rather than cooking.

The doorbell rang while she was rinsing off her lunch dishes. She wasn't expecting anyone, but life at the Shafer Farm meant visitors—expected or not. She tightened her ponytail and smoothed her shirt over her round belly. She checked the window on her way to the door.

"Hi, Angela." The man held an old banker's box.

"What a nice surprise!" Angela replied. This was Donna's son, she remembered that much, but his name escaped her. "Um, it's good to see you . . . ?" She gave him a knowing but searching look.

"Oh, it's Eric. I'm—"

"Of course. Eric. It's this pregnancy brain, sorry. I'm lucky if I can remember my own name some days. Please, come in." She moved out of the doorway. He stepped inside with the box, and as soon as he set it down, he went back to the porch to bring in another.

"What do we have here?" Angela asked, trying to keep the concern out of her voice.

"A few things we found in our basement that belong to you."

Angela could see faded words scrawled along the side of the box: *Shaf. Fm. Christmas Decor.*

"What do you know—more Christmas decorations," she said, forcing cheerfulness.

"Apparently." Eric grinned. "My wife went through them to make sure. She said it looks like my mom probably packed them up from the farm one year. We're not sure if it was before or after the fire."

Angela watched Donna's son as he spoke. He had an easy way about him, and even when he mentioned his mother, there was a slight smile around his eyes. By the look of the boxes, the decorations had to be pretty old. Angela didn't think they needed more Christmas decorations, but it was kind of Eric to bring the boxes over.

"Are you sure your family doesn't want them? Are they things your mom made?"

Eric lifted the lid of the first box to inspect the top layer of its contents. "We have a lot of my mom's crafts, that's for sure." He shrugged his shoulders. "My wife went through it. She said it all belonged to the farm. I'm sorry we didn't know it was left in the basement."

"No need to apologize. Thanks for making the trip. Please tell Cynthia she needs to come over with the kids soon," Angela said, relieved she remembered his wife's name.

"Will do," Eric said before excusing himself.

Angela closed the door and let out a heavy sigh. Just when she thought she'd made progress in her declutter project, two more boxes needed a home. She approached one and looked at the writing on the side again.

Christmas Decor? She shook her head. *Donna's Barn had an unlimited supply of decorations, didn't it?* Well, it seemed so. At least on opening day it was full to overflowing.

"What's a few more holiday crafts for a tree farm?" she mumbled to herself as she bent down and rummaged through the contents. Pain shot across her back as she was picking up some old handmade stockings. She closed her eyes and tried to breathe. Another pain followed. She opened her eyes and straightened up. Maybe she'd reached her limit for the day. She pressed her hands into her lower back and took a few more breaths. The pain was gone, but a soreness lingered. She eyed the boxes sitting there and pressed her lips together.

I didn't work all day to end up with more clutter lying around.

She pushed one box against the wall with her foot, then did the same to the second box.

"Hey, I'm back. What are you doing over there?" Mark's voice called from the side door.

"You're just in time," she said.

"For what, exactly?" Mark asked as he approached, pulling her into a hug.

She leaned into him and let her forehead rest on his shoulder. His closeness and warmth eased her tension a bit. He rubbed the small of her back as if he knew how sore it was. She forgot entirely why she was standing near the front door.

"Are you okay?" He searched her face. "What are these boxes? Have you been doing too much? I can't leave you alone with this house, can I?"

"No, I'm fine. These are from Eric. You just missed him," Angela said. "He said they found them in their basement. They think Donna packed them up one year, and they wanted us to have them." She gave a somewhat defeated sigh.

"What's wrong?" Mark asked, still examining her more than the boxes.

Angela burst into tears. Ugh, so unlike her. She felt betrayed by her pregnant body. "More clutter, Mark. I spent most of the morning sorting the baby's room. I finally tackled the closet," she said between sobs she couldn't control.

"Hey, come sit down."

"No, I'm okay," she insisted. "I wanted to finish the room before we went out tonight. Can you do something with these boxes? Find a place for them, or better yet, go through them and—" She broke down in another fit of sobs.

"Shh, it's okay. Consider it done. I'll take them to the cabin. How's that? Out of sight." He pulled her in for a hug.

"Oh, ow." She felt another pain, this time across her abdomen.

"Sorry, too tight?" Mark asked as he immediately released her.

"No. Maybe. I don't know. Probably more Braxton Hicks, that's all."

"You have overdone it. That settles it. You go rest. I'll get you something to eat."

"Mark, you don't have to do that. I had a roast beef and cheese sandwich for lunch." She met his eyes, full of concern for her but also a flicker of another emotion. Was that a wince? He gave her a half-smile.

"You're sick of roast beef," she stated rather than asked.

She thought she saw fear in his eyes as he paused for a moment. They both broke out laughing.

"Maybe a little," he said.

"Three nights in a row is too much, huh?" She laughed, releasing all the tension she didn't know was still stored up.

"Four, but who's counting?" Mark shot back.

"My guess is we aren't going out for steak tonight?"

"No. That much I can tell you. Unless you're telling me that's the only thing you can eat. If so, we have a problem," he said.

Angela headed toward the master bedroom while Mark turned back toward the kitchen. She looked over her shoulder. "Aren't you forgetting something?" she asked as she nodded toward the boxes on the floor, a teasing smile on her face.

"Oh, right," Mark said. "Boxes. Cabin. Right away."

He got as far as the cash register when Angela let out a yelp from the end of the hallway. He dropped the boxes at his feet and rushed to her side.

❄

She protested all the way to the hospital, insisting the pain wasn't as bad as she made it sound. She was worn out, that was all. She complained they didn't need another hospital bill. Mark said he wouldn't stop worrying until the doctor told him there was nothing to worry about. Even as he parked the car and came around and opened her door, she sat there, unmoving. She restated that she didn't want another embarrassing encounter, but there was no dissuading him. Their playful laughter over roast beef had evaporated. Once Mark made up his mind, Angela didn't stand a chance of changing it.

For better or worse, the nurse who had helped Angela at her last visit was on duty. She greeted them kindly and took Angela to an observation bed. She was connected to monitors in no time. Mark sat in the chair and held her hand, though she felt more annoyed than comforted. She had about thirty minutes' worth of contractions, but the sharpest one was the first in the hallway. The rest hadn't been nearly as painful. The longer she stayed in the hospital bed, the better she felt. Rather, the more determined she felt that she was fine and that this would end up the same way the last visit had.

When the nurse reappeared, Angela asked if she was free to go. She sat up, hoping to be able to walk right out the door. "We've got reservations. Tell her, Mark. I need to go home and get ready."

"Not so fast, Mrs. Shafer. We've paged the doctor on call, and he will want to see you."

That wasn't what Angela wanted to hear.

"I'll call the restaurant," Mark said before stepping out of the exam room.

When he returned, Angela waited before she spoke. "Well?" she finally asked.

"Well, what?"

"How long will they hold the reservation?"

"Hold it? I asked them to cancel it. You heard the nurse. We're waiting for the doctor, and we have no idea what he'll tell us."

"So, I am stuck in this hospital and will miss whatever surprise you had planned?" Angela felt a sob starting in her chest. She threw up her hands, resigned to all things pregnant conspiring against her. She cried and laughed at the same time, probably confusing Mark.

"I'm sorry, we'll go another time. The restaurant isn't going anywhere."

"Apparently, neither am I!" she joked. "You know, if you really wanted the cafeteria's Saturday-night special, you could have just said so. No need to drag me here as an excuse."

❄

Three hours later, they drove home in silence. Mark had already said he was sorry, twice, and twice Angela had replied she was okay. Although she wasn't sure if that was true. Yes, the doctor had confirmed what she'd predicted—more false labor pains. That was the good news. The not-so-great-news was she had become dehydrated and needed fluids. She would need to be more careful to not let it happen again. No matter how long Angela was pregnant, she could not get used to how out of control she felt at times. In one day, she'd overworked herself due to some crazy nesting instinct, sobbed uncontrollably in Mark's arms over a pair of boxes, and ended up dehydrated and needing medical help. Mark had been right to insist on the hospital, though that was little comfort when she thought of the anniversary they were supposed to be celebrating.

"What did I miss?" Angela asked.

"Come again?"

"The restaurant, the reservation? Do I get to know why I needed to wear something dressy?"

She watched Mark's eyes dart to her and back to the road.

"What? You mean holding hands in the maternity department wasn't your idea of a romantic night out?" Mark joked.

"Let's see. Florescent lights, hooked up to monitors, dinner from the cafeteria . . ." she began.

"At least it was nacho night."

". . . is not, could never be, romantic."

"I don't know . . . you got to sport a *gown*."

She hit his shoulder. "Don't you dare say what I looked like in it."

"Gorgeous."

"Stop," Angela said.

"Ravishing," Mark countered.

"Enough."

"How about *glowing*?" he teased.

She hit his shoulder again. "You're insufferable, you know that."

They pulled up to the farmhouse, and Mark helped Angela out of the truck. She didn't let go of his hand. On the porch, he leaned down and kissed her.

"I'll make sure we celebrate our anniversary properly," Mark said.

Once again, tears sprung to her eyes. All she could do was wipe them away before her cheeks became chapped. She nodded a thank-you to Mark, choosing not to talk for fear of sobs escaping instead of words.

Why this pregnancy proved to be more challenging than her first, other than it was over twelve years later, she couldn't say. But she was beginning to look forward to delivering this baby and reclaiming a little more control over her emotions.

CHAPTER 8

Angela had long been asleep, something Mark couldn't do no matter how he'd tried. He was haunted by the look of disappointment on her face when he told her he'd canceled their reservation. As if missing the surprise dinner he'd planned wasn't bad enough, Angela had to endure another trip to the hospital. Her labor had been false, but the dehydration had been very real. And she'd worked hard again, too hard, getting things ready for this baby.

The boxes she'd been so upset about were still by the cash register. She had cried over them—a pregnancy symptom, he was sure. Yet, if he could sort them and stash them somewhere out of sight, that would be one less thing to cause her tears. Despite the late hour, doing something with those boxes from Donna's house was at least something he could do for her. He might feel less helpless too. Even if it meant sorting old farm items that could trigger memories of his parents.

A few years ago, he would have loved to have anything that survived the fire that claimed his parents' lives. But now that he was married to Angela and about to have a son, he wasn't as drawn to the past. Old boxes didn't have the same magnetic pull they once did. Angela had worn herself weary cleaning the house and decorating the baby's room and making sure there wasn't a diaper, book, or rattle out of place. He could do this for her.

The first box contained red, felt stockings. They hardly looked like they could hold anything and must have been purely for show. The names *Mom* and *Pop* and *Greg* were stitched on the white felt edges. He held them for a moment as he thought of his dad as a boy before setting them aside. He dug deeper through layers of imitation popcorn garland.

No wonder this was in Donna's basement.

He kept out the stockings, but the garland was too old to keep. By the time he opened the second box, Mark felt like he had hit a groove. He could finish soon and still get a few hours of sleep before sunrise. He pulled all the contents out to sort everything more quickly. One box he allocated for items to keep, the other for items to give away, like old pine-cone ornaments. Something unusual caught his eye. Was it a quilt? He unfolded it and held it up. Too small for a bed, and round. There was a hole in the center.

Maybe it wasn't finished, he thought as he examined a seam that looked like it needed to be sewn. He was about to fold it back up when it struck him. It was a tree skirt.

At first glance, it seemed much older than almost everything else in the boxes. Clearly well-made to have lasted this long, but soft and delicate too. The colors were vibrant red and green, though the white had yellowed some. Definitely handmade, and though quilts were not Mark's specialty, he knew enough of quality that he was sure Angela would want to keep it for their family. Before he could move it to the keep box, he held it close and studied the stitches. Some of them sparkled.

"Gold thread," he said out loud, fascinated by the shimmer in the fabric.

Probably wasn't cheap back in the day.

Another item in the box sparkled like the skirt. He picked up what looked like a small, star-shaped pillow—only it wasn't exactly a pillow. He turned it over and compared it to the skirt. The fabric was the same, and the center of the tree skirt had a star-shaped opening that matched the pillow. He studied both, holding them up and turning them over. The backside of the star had two ribbons. It could be tied to the top of the tree, and the quilt was a tree skirt for the floor. A matching set.

He wanted to keep it out of the box and show Angela, but he remembered Angela's current state of mind. No clutter, no extraneous items, and her recent declaration: if the baby doesn't need it, neither do we!

He placed the tree skirt and the star topper in the keep box. Soon he had the lids on both boxes and moved them to the other side of the hallway. He went in search of a permanent marker to label them but gave up once he saw the time. He grabbed a drink of water and planned to mark them in the morning—not too many hours away.

He opened the hall closet and quietly shuffled a few things to fit both boxes. He wasn't going to trek to the cabin after midnight, but at least this way, Angela would not see them when she woke up.

❋

Carl left Mark a message, notifying him he could start Monday. Mark should not have been surprised to see Carl pull up at 6:30 a.m. Other workers wouldn't have shown up until seven, and though he and Papa had already been on a short walk, it was still early by anyone's standards.

Papa approved of Mark's choice of calling Carl. "Family is good for the farm, and the farm is good for family," he said.

"We'll see," Mark said, a hint of skepticism in his voice.

They all shook hands at the edge of the parking lot. Mark brought Carl up to speed on how many trees they had staged and how many more they hoped to cut and transport to the sales lot. Though the temperatures had been some of the coldest in years, they'd been spared the heavy snows of previous ones. They wouldn't have to fight the snow while they cut and loaded more trees.

"We need to move another twenty or thirty today."

"Consider it done," Carl said.

"What about the balers and shakers?" Papa asked.

"I haven't had a chance to inspect those yet. Could you take a look at them and let me know if they need any fine-tuning?" Mark asked Papa.

"Is that it?" Carl asked.

"I wish. If the wind leaves us alone today, we can put more lights up at Donna's barn," Mark said.

"Great. Can never have too many of those."

"We probably already do." Mark chuckled. "Dorothy and Angela got together and decided to have extra lights for the trail leading to it, as well as the sides. We might confuse small aircraft by the time we're done."

They all shared a laugh, and then Papa headed toward the equipment while Mark and Carl walked to the lot of balsam firs.

"Hey, why do you call it Donna's Barn if Dorothy is the one who runs it? Who's Donna?" Carl asked.

Mark's jaw stiffened before he answered. "Donna ran the barn before Dorothy. She died a few years ago, and we named the barn after her. You know, to honor her."

"She worked here awhile?" Carl asked.

"You could say that. Thirty years, give or take. She was family. Best friends with my mom."

They'd reached the first section of trees just in time. Mark wasn't in the mood for any more questions. Carl went right to work with only a few pointers from Mark. No one could compare to Brett, but Carl was focused and efficient. The sun was up, and though the temperature was still low, the bright sunlight warmed Mark's cheeks and forehead.

Fifteen trees had been cut and stacked for transport. Mark suggested they take a small break. He grabbed the backpack he'd brought and offered Carl water and a protein bar.

"What do you sell more of, the balsam or Fraser?" Carl asked between bites.

"Hard to say. Probably the balsam. It has a distinct fragrance customers like. Papa likes to sell the Douglas or Scotch pines. We get fewer customer complaints with those because they hold their needles."

"What about blue spruce?"

"Oh, sure, we need to have some of those. Parents with little ones like them."

Carl seemed confused.

"When you grab one, it grabs you back. Parents tell me their kids learn pretty quick to leave the tree alone."

"Well, what do you know? Hadn't heard that one before."

"Customers love to share," Mark said.

"True. And just wait until your regulars see Angela. My guess is you'll have a lot of back-slapping this season."

Mark hadn't thought of that, but Carl was right. Just as some customers had returned with small gifts after they'd found out Mark and Angela had gotten married, they would definitely be excited over this baby on the way.

"Before you know it, your son will be working right alongside you."

It was an offhand remark. Mark knew Carl meant nothing by it, but in an instant, Mark missed his dad. Not something he thought about or dwelled on very much. As he imagined his own son learning to work the farm, a cascade of emotions followed.

Would his son want to work with him? Would his son want to take over for him one day?

These questions wouldn't have answers for at least two more decades. Mark hoped his son would come to love the trees as much as he did, but he wouldn't force him. He'd have a choice.

"Hey, was it something I said?" Carl asked, taking note of Mark's silence.

"What? It's nothing. Let's cut this last row, and then we can head back."

Transporting the trees, grabbing lunch, and staging the barn lights went as quickly and smoothly as Mark had hoped. If this was how Carl worked every day—as opposed to putting on a good show for the first day—Mark wouldn't have any reason to worry about opening weekend. He could do without the personal questions, but he had to admit Carl was a hard worker.

They had a few more strings to hang when Mark's phone rang.

Angela.

"Hey, how are you feeling today?" he asked.

"Fine," she answered, but she had a different reason for calling. She'd gone looking for a tablecloth for Thanksgiving she kept in the hall closet.

"Why are the boxes still in the house?"

The boxes. He'd totally forgotten.

"I sorted through them last night but didn't want to hike to the cabin. Listen, I'll take care of them when I'm done here."

"I'm ready to take care of them now," she told him.

"Okay, one is ready to be donated. The other has some things we need to keep."

"One box can go?" Angela asked.

"Yes, but the other one that has stockings and a quilt—that one needs to stay."

"You're sure we need to keep it? Any idea where it can go? Can we put it in a newer box?"

Three questions in a row meant Mark had about ten seconds to convince her this was not a crisis. Just one little box.

"I'm sorry. I will take care of them as soon as I get back. I'll find a place, I prom—"

"No need. Tell me again which one goes and which one stays. I'm on my way into town," she said.

Mark described the contents of the box to keep but insisted Angela did not need to worry about them.

"I'll take care of it," he repeated.

When he hung up, he thought about going inside right away, but he looked at Carl and the lights. Two hands were better than one. They'd finish, and he'd return before Angela did anything drastic.

CHAPTER 9

Angela lifted the lids on both boxes. She had no patience for sorting them. She trusted that Mark had been thorough. One box was to keep, and the other was to give away. Simple. She quickly assessed both boxes, replaced the lids, and grabbed the box they needed to keep. She knew exactly where it could go and could not move it fast enough. She opened the door to a squeal from across the room.

She marched to Donna's barn to find Dorothy.

"What do we have here? Someone who shouldn't be working this hard." Dorothy answered her own question with a disapproving look.

"It's only a box. Mark already sorted it. I'd hardly call it work," Angela defended herself. "He said this is the box we need to keep."

"Keep it here?" Dorothy asked as she stared at the box.

Angela picked it up and carried it to the back room, not waiting for Dorothy to agree.

"One less box in the house means I will sleep better tonight," she said as she returned to the front counter. Dorothy hadn't moved. In fact, she was staring quite intently at Angela.

"You feeling okay, dear?" she asked.

Angela felt like she got a glimpse of herself through Dorothy's eyes, and the image startled her.

"Am I becoming like my mother?" Angela asked, alarm in her voice.

"That's a tricky question. A bit of nesting is nothing to fuss about. Besides, your mother is a fine woman."

"You know what I mean. Have I become an intolerable organizer?"

Dorothy sighed. "If you start alphabetizing your spice jars, I'll stage a—what do they call them? An intervention."

"Hmm. Hadn't thought of that," Angela said. "Guess I can take comfort in that."

Angela was anxious to go, but Dorothy had one of those earnest expressions.

"What is it? What's bothering you?" Dorothy asked. "Are you feeling okay?"

"Mark asks me that often. Yes, I am okay." She furrowed her brow and rubbed the side of her belly. Glancing around the craft barn, she noticed the pine-bough wreaths, village houses, and ice-skating figurines lining the wall shelf. It was as if she'd never seen them before.

Sometimes she had to remind herself that she'd married a Christmas-tree farmer.

"You know what I think it is? As different as my life was all those years ago when I was married to Todd, being pregnant again hasn't just brought back the memories, it's brought back the insecurities," Angela said, returning her attention to Dorothy and the shelf she was organizing.

"Like what?"

"Where do I start?" Angela lamented.

"How about handing me another two Santa cookie trays from the box?"

Angela complied, though still thinking about how to answer Dorothy's question.

"Go ahead. What insecurities are troubling you?" she asked.

"Let's see. The last time I was pregnant, my husband found a pretty little band member to rehearse with, and my mother had not only stopped talking to me, she refused any and all help unless I moved back home."

Dorothy stacked the trays on the shelf and motioned for a few more. "I see. Not a happy time, to be sure, and not your mother's finest hour. But you can see the difference. That was a long time ago. And Mark, well, he would never."

"You're right," Angela said. "I know Mark. I trust him. He's being so attentive, which makes it all the more irrational that I fear this baby will change our relationship." Angela let out a sigh. "And my mother, she's not threatening to disown me again, but she is swooping in and spending more time with Caroline."

"Let me get this straight," Dorothy started. "Your mother and your husband are being supportive and loving, and you still feel like you're at risk of sudden abandonment, all because of a baby on the way?"

Angela understood why Dorothy suppressed a grin. "I'm ridiculous, aren't I?"

"No, it sounds like par for the course, my dear. If our emotions were logical, well, they wouldn't be emotions, would they? Seems to me if you could survive that terrible time with your loved ones letting you down, you ought to be able to find a way of putting up with a little bit of smothering."

She said it with her no-fuss British accent, which comforted Angela and settled the matter in one smooth stroke. At least for now.

"What are you going to do about it?" Dorothy asked.

"Funny you should ask. I'm headed into town. Do you need anything?"

"Not at all. What's in town that can't wait for Mark?"

"If I waited for Mark, this would never get done," Angela said, gesturing to the back, where she'd planted the first box. She quickly clamped her mouth shut. She wasn't going to complain to Dorothy about Mark, even if he was working so long that he was sleep-walking through the door when he got home. She wasn't going to be that kind of wife.

Dorothy didn't need an explanation. "Sorry. I shouldn't have suggested that. I know the farm is claiming all his time."

"It's no bother. I like the drive, and it will do me some good. See you later."

❄

Angela loaded the box into the back of her truck. She stared at it for a moment. If she was going to Goodwill, she might as well find a few more things to take. She'd already gone through her clothes in the last few months but couldn't pass up the chance to make more room in her closet. It would be some time before she could make another trip.

❄

Angela handed the bag full of clothes she knew she'd never wear again to the man at the donation door of Goodwill. He was appreciative, and she was relieved to know she'd gotten rid of more clutter. Relieved was putting it mildly. Ecstatic? Elated? Yes, that too.

Was this the way her mother felt? With intense emotions coursing through her just because she was off-loading more clutter, she wondered if she had misunderstood her mother. Maybe it wasn't completely about control. Maybe her mother enjoyed it. Was it possible it brought her joy? Or freedom? Was that such a bad thing?

Another reason for Angela to be kinder.

That was the thought running through Angela's mind when her mother called. *Be kind*, she reminded herself. *How hard can it be?*

"I'm here at your house. Where are you?" she asked, though it sounded like a bark.

"Let's see. Downtown Sutton," Angela replied cautiously.

"You said you were decluttering today."

"I was."

"Well, you couldn't have gotten much done if you're out and about now."

Angela abandoned her *be kind* mantra and opted for *don't lose it*.

"Mom, why, uh, why are you at my house?" Not that Angela really wanted to know, but it was the best chance she had at changing the subject.

"For Caroline. I'm here to pick Caroline up, and she isn't here either."

"I'm picking her up from school on my way home."

Angela's reply was met with silence. This told Angela her mother had likely forgotten her granddaughter attended something as ordinary as junior high and couldn't be at her beck and call.

"Was there something you needed? We'll be home in about thirty minutes," Angela said, grateful for how calm she felt.

"Yes. I need Caroline. I promised her she could go with me again."

Promised? Without talking to me? So much for those calm feelings. "I didn't know the plan. Maybe a heads-up next time?"

"We didn't find anything suitable for the charity auction, and Caroline asked to go with me. She said she even had some stores in mind where I could find some real 'gems,' I think she called them," Cathy said.

"She'll have homework. Do you know how long your shopping trip will be?"

"No. I don't. As long as it takes. But as her grandmother, I would think you'd trust me more than that accusing tone in your voice suggests."

Angela sighed, not caring if her mother heard it. "You know what, I think it's a great idea. If Caroline has some places in mind for the two of you, I hope you find what you're looking for."

There. She'd sidestepped the trigger, bypassed the urge to argue, and expressed a genuine thought instead. It may have taken every ounce of her recent resolve to be kind, but she did it.

Angela returned to the farmhouse with Caroline to find Cathy in her kitchen. The cupboards were open, and she was rummaging for what, Angela could only imagine.

She stood on the threshold and, with a deep inhale, summoned what patience she had left.

"Mom, Caroline's here. Aren't you two going shopping?" This was an effort to redirect.

"Hmm" was the only sound from Cathy as she studied one of the lower cupboards with her back to Angela.

Soon Cathy shook her head. "This won't do."

"What *won't do*? Are you looking for something?"

Cathy turned and faced Angela with a how-could-you-not-know expression.

"Your dishes, for starters. How can you serve dinner to seven people on Corelle? Is it still seven? That's an odd amount of people, you know. First things first. I know you have china. I gave it to you. You didn't sell it, did you?"

Angela walked calmly to one end of the kitchen and began closing the cabinets. One at a time.

"Remember our agreement?" Angela asked.

"No. What are you talking about? Where is the china?"

Angela couldn't tell if her mother was too caught up in her china-plate obsession to remember or if she was purposely denying their conversation.

"If you come as a guest to our Thanksgiving dinner, you're not in charge—that's what it means to be a guest," Angela reminded her.

"Who said anything about being in charge? I'm simply helping you find the china so you'll be ready. I could set the table before we go, as a practice run. Those are particularly helpful. You must see the way the light reflects the colors in your tablecloth. It could overwhelm the dishes, and if you need to buy different linens, there is still time. Though not a very good selection."

"No. There will be no more buying of different anything. Seriously, the light and colors? Who pays attention to that?" Angela remembered who she was talking to. "We're not doing a practice run." Unbidden memories of after-school table-setting practice reinforced Angela's resolve to say no.

Cathy's eyes reflected that mix of confusion and hurt.

"Besides, Caroline is waiting to go with you. It's a school night," Angela quickly added.

"I see," Cathy said, gingerly wiping her hands on the sides of her dress pants. "We'll go," she said as she moved out of the kitchen, her gaze straight ahead.

Angela felt that familiar tug at her heart.

How does she do it? Make me feel like I'm the bad guy?

"I didn't sell the china," she called out.

She stood in the kitchen for a moment. She could hear Cathy and Caroline putting on their coats by the front door. She didn't feel the need to see them off, and she didn't feel any need to say she was sorry. Yet, as she heard the front door close and stood alone in the middle of her kitchen, she glared at the cupboards. "I may not know where it is, but I didn't sell the china."

CHAPTER 10

Mark walked the trees at dawn. A storm had moved through the farm overnight and left a heavy blanket of snow. The trees were quiet, and each step he took felt new. He looked behind him to see the trail he'd created. One set of footprints today. He thought of Papa, of his dad, and of the son he had on the way.

Maybe one day, his footsteps will match mine.

Outside, all was still in the predawn light, but inside, Mark's thoughts were clashing. He forced them to quiet down and finished his walk.

Carl had worked hard and helped Mark in every way he'd needed, yet he couldn't shake the not-quite-right feeling he had about him. He also felt an echo of dread, like he'd felt on Tree Choosing Day. His thoughts turned to Angela and the false labor she'd been having. His stomach tightened. His concern for her well-being had become his constant companion.

There's a change coming.

Be ready.

The words breezed through his mind. If Papa or anyone else had said them, he would have asked what they were talking about. But they were his thoughts, and he knew what they meant. He needed to pay attention and be ready to keep the trees safe.

By the time Mark reached the side door to the farmhouse, Carl had arrived, even earlier than before. It was the day before Thanksgiving, two days before they officially opened, and while the necessary work had been finished, some things needed attention. Like that stubborn flocking machine that kept losing power and snow removal from the overnight snowstorm. Eight inches hadn't buried them, but it was plenty to make a mess if they didn't get to work and clean it up.

Mark and Carl worked in tandem, clearing the snow off the trails to the sales lot and to Donna's barn and the farmhouse. A cloudless sky allowed the winter sun to shine. The snow glistened, not merely reflecting the sunlight but transforming it into dazzling white glitter. Mark had worked up a sweat and an appetite. Usually, it was Brett threatening to strike if Mark wouldn't stop for lunch. Carl, on the other hand, seemed to be willing to work right through it.

They had meatball sandwiches ready for them in the kitchen.

"Does your family cook a turkey?" Mark asked. "Or something else?"

"Oh, yeah, all the usual sides too."

Mark could see a shadow cross Carl's face. He hesitated, but it felt like the right thing to do.

"Do you have plans for tomorrow?" Once the words left Mark's mouth, he realized he hadn't even talked to Angela. Maybe they had plans already.

"Yeah, well, sort of. Penny's brother-in-law is in the hospital again with another infection that isn't responding to antibiotics."

Mark nodded and took another bite of his sandwich.

Carl continued. "The plan was a family dinner, nothing too big. But Penny's sister decided she wanted to wait till he's home and then have a big meal."

"But not tomorrow?"

"Probably not for another week."

"Then you and Penny bring the kids and come join us," Mark said, feeling confident Angela would agree.

"Oh no, we couldn't." Carl shook his head and looked around the kitchen. "We're not here to intrude. From what Penny tells me, Angela has to take it easy."

"It's Thanksgiving, and we're cousins. I'm pretty sure Angela and Caroline will be thrilled for you to come. What about your sister-in-law's kids?"

"Two boys, older than ours and much better behaved."

"Yep. Bring them too."

"They'll be with their parents at the hospital," Carl said quickly. "Listen, I don't know what to say."

"Say yes. We eat at two. I'll let Angela know, and she'll probably give Penny a call."

After she lets me have it for inviting five more people to dinner. He laughed to himself.

"We better finish up the parking lot," Mark said.

❄

Mark rubbed his stiffening shoulders as he walked down the hall. Caroline was sound asleep, so he turned off the extra hall light. He thought he heard Angela in the kitchen, but he was sure she'd finished all the day-before Thanksgiving prep with Dorothy. Maybe she had a late-night craving and was grabbing a snack.

The pies should be taste-tested, he thought. *Maybe the apple or the pumpkin.*

He entered the kitchen and found Angela sitting on the floor cross-legged, all the cabinets empty and her hair looking like she'd had a tug-of-war with it. Not sure why the kitchen would be the target of her nesting instinct, but here she was.

"Hey, what's with all the dishes?"

"Corelle. You mean Corelle dishes. Ordinary, average ones. Prosaic, actually, but that word is too fancy to describe my garden-variety plates."

"O—kay. How about I help you put them back?" Mark carefully stepped around her and replaced a stack of bowls. Angela was muttering to herself about her mother and a wedding registry.

"We didn't have a registry."

"Not one we agreed to. My mother set one up for us."

"Without your permission?" Mark asked, continuing to restock the cabinets.

"Permission, ha! She did it without my knowledge. Told her friends and everything."

"Not that it matters, but why am I hearing about this now? It's been a few years," Mark asked.

"China, that's why."

Mark straightened up. "As in the country? What does—"

"As in the dishware. She gave us a truckload of it, and I have no idea where it is." She used both hands to pull her hair behind her shoulders, wrapping the ends up in a tight bun and letting it fall loose again.

Mark let a smile slip. She was cute when she was flustered and she exaggerated, but he knew enough to not tell her either of those things at the moment.

"You don't have to find the plates this minute, do you?" he asked.

"You mean the fine china." She threw her hands in the air. "And yes, I do. Thanksgiving is tomorrow! If I don't have my mother's gift opened and in use, we will never hear the end of it."

Thanksgiving. It wasn't like Mark forgot what was happening tomorrow, but he and Carl and Papa had worked through sundown. Angela had gone to town with Dorothy for one more trip to the grocery store while he had a late dinner alone.

And he'd forgotten to tell her.

He took a deep breath and exhaled slowly. "About tomorrow—I invited Carl and Penny."

Angela glared at him. He shifted his weight against the counter, then tossed his head back and stared at the ceiling, thoughts racing about how he could make this up to her.

"I was going to tell you right after lunch, but I got a call," he started explaining.

"Mark," she said sharply.

"Dorothy is helping you, and Caroline will too, I'm sure. Maybe she and Macie will both help," he said.

"I know."

"We can have a table for the kids."

"I know," she repeated.

Mark looked at her smirk and realized she *knew*—as in already knew they were coming.

"How?"

"Penny called."

"So, you're not mad?" He had to at least check.

"I should be since you're telling me at, what, nine thirty at night."

"Sorry, but does this mean we're good?"

"Not unless we find Cathy's china."

"Right." Mark began looking in all the cabinets he had just filled with the dishes Angela had moved out. "Do you have any idea where did you put it?"

"Evidently nowhere in this kitchen." She stood and slowly closed the cabinet doors. Her eyes swept the kitchen, still half torn up from her frenzied search.

"Why wouldn't you put them in here?" Worn out and with no motivation to track down a never-used wedding gift, Mark rubbed his forehead.

"I never thought I'd use expensive dishes. Want to guess how much they cost? Don't answer that. I'm sure I thought they needed a good hiding place."

Mark searched his memory. A box of dishes wouldn't be small. "I don't know where to start, unless you left yourself a note. You've already cleaned half this house."

"True," she said.

"Can we call it a night and I'll help you find them in the morning? I have just enough steam to fall into bed."

"Wait. That's it!" She took off down the hall.

Mark followed, unsure what she meant, only to find her wrestling a box out from under their bed.

"Let me get that before you pull something."

"There should be three more," she said.

"Four boxes? How many plates did she give us?"

"Service for eight." Angela was tapping her thumb to each finger, counting in her head. "Twenty-four plates including the small ones."

"Twenty-four plates for eight people?"

"Courses. Remember, my mother loves her courses."

❆

Angela gently pulled one of the plates from its protective sleeve and held it up for Mark to see. "Twenty-four-karat-gold accents," she said.

"Don't tell me those are rubies."

"Yep, small ones. They're enameled or something." She ran her fingers over the herringbone design. The scroll-and-leaf motif caught her eye. It was not the same as her mother's pattern, but similar. She abruptly put the plate back in the sleeve.

"What is it?" Mark asked.

"Nothing."

"That was *something*."

"Fine. I like the pattern."

Mark didn't need to know that this was the first time Angela had actually looked at the plates. Or that she was only now realizing what her mother had done. He didn't need to know about the shopping trip they'd taken before Angela's first wedding. That they had argued over everything except the china pattern. Even though Angela had loved it, she wouldn't accept the gift from her mother. She and Todd were going to be in an apartment, and Angela refused to have $1,000 dishes in the kitchen.

Angela felt a small smile emerge. Her mother had gifted them the pattern Angela liked—not the pattern her mother wanted, not the latest trend, not the most expensive—the one design Angela had told her once, and only once, that she liked.

That was over ten years before her wedding to Mark. How could her mother have remembered?

She closed the box and looked up to see Mark staring at her.

"Are you going to tell me what it is about the china that has you a million miles away? Or should I ask your mom?"

Angela squared her shoulders.

"She knew I'd like them. That's all."

CHAPTER 11

Once Angela had found the lost china, or the forgot-where-she'd-stashed-it china, she began looking forward to the holiday. Her mother would be pleased, or maybe appeased, that Angela had kept the gift. There would be enough dishes for all four of the couples that would be seated at the dining room table. She also knew with Dorothy's focus in the kitchen, the food would be fine. No pots boiling over, no burning the rolls. Nothing got past Dorothy.

Penny was coming too. She was easy to talk to and willing to share all her baby tips. She'd also offered to arrive early to help so Angela could put her feet up. But that wasn't about to happen.

This was their first Thanksgiving meal at the farmhouse since being married, and she wasn't going to sit it out and miss the fun. In the previous two years, her mother had demanded they come to her house, claiming they were always at the farm for Christmas. This year, Angela had declared rather defiantly that they would be having Thanksgiving dinner at her home. Cathy and Gary could come or not, and if Cathy did choose to come, she had to agree to be a guest, not a manager.

It had been one of Angela's small victories. It had also happened before she knew she was having a baby. Whatever stress she felt over hosting the dinner was offset by the comfort of being in her own home.

I can put my feet up after dinner, she reasoned.

She entered the dark kitchen, where the chilly air greeted her. She preheated the oven but left the lights off. The house would become busy, bright, and loud soon enough, so, for a moment, she reveled in the stillness, peering through the window over the sink. Tomorrow they would share the trees and the farm with all the friends who came, but today they could have it to themselves. Good food, family, and the trees surrounding them.

"What's going on in here?" Mark appeared at her side to wrap his arms around her without turning on the lights.

She tilted her head into his shoulder, relaxing into his warmth. "Checking on the trees."

"That's my job," Mark said protectively.

"You don't have exclusive rights to feeling thankful for them."

"True." He kissed her cheek and lingered there.

"This might be my only chance for a moment of gratitude."

"Good morning, Mom. Hi, Mark! Happy Thanksgiving!" Caroline flipped the lights on. "Whatcha doing in the dark?"

"See what I mean?" she said to Mark as she pulled Caroline in for a quick side hug.

"Your mom was having a moment of silence. Enjoying the calm before the storm."

"I was having a thankful moment for the trees." She gave Mark a pointed look. "And for our family. That's what you do on a day like today."

"And eat. We are going to cook a turkey, right?" Caroline shot back.

Mark laughed. Angela sighed but chuckled too. "Yes, we will eat."

"Can I be in charge of the stuffing this year? I like it with carrots and onions but not raisins."

"Your grandmother likes raisins."

"I know, and those dried cranberries too, but come on, if dinner is at our house, don't we get to call the shots?"

Angela and Mark exchanged a quick glance.

"That's one way of looking at it," Mark said.

"If dinner is at our house, it means we get to think about making it nice for our guests," Angela instructed.

Caroline was already rummaging around for baking dishes. She held up one and then another. "Fine. I'll make both kinds. One pan of the good stuff and another with all the icky things."

"Good luck," Mark said as he gave Angela a quick kiss. "I've got to be on the sales lot in five."

"Why the sales lot?" she asked.

"I'm meeting Papa. We're bringing home the tree from the six-year lot, remember?" Mark said as he was headed for the door.

The tree!

How could she have forgotten? The plan had been to decorate it after dinner, with everyone who came. Between meeting Carl and Penny, the false labor scare, and searching for the china, she *had* forgotten their favorite tradition. She left the kitchen in search of the ornaments and lights for the tree.

When she returned, Dorothy had arrived and had the kitchen set up, staged, and was putting the turkey in the oven. She was even supervising Caroline and her two-batch stuffing operation. If it were anyone else, Angela might have felt displaced, but this was Dorothy, and her chatter put Angela at ease. Besides, Dorothy wasn't doing everything. Angela had a knack for baking homemade rolls with a recipe she'd finessed from one of her mother's chefs. Her concentration on perfecting the rolls may have been the reason she didn't catch it at first. Dorothy had seemed like her usual busy self, but a comment here and a near cuss word there, and it struck Angela—she was irritated.

She wanted to come right out and ask why, but with Caroline in between them, that conversation would have to wait.

Before long, Penny arrived with Carl and their children. Caroline grabbed Macie as soon as she came through the door, and they disappeared to Caroline's room. Angela could have asked Dorothy what was bothering her, but it still wasn't the right time with Penny there.

Angela quickly discovered how much you could learn about someone when you cooked together. Penny announced she liked leaving the skin on her carrots. Dorothy stated the carrots would be properly peeled and chopped. Penny declared the turkey needed to be cooked upside down, allowing the breast meat to soak up the juices. Dorothy countered that she'd installed Mr. Turkey in the oven right side up, and there would be no flipping him over. She'd said it in a cordial, no-hard-feelings way, but she also added a quick wave of her hand and a nod of her head—meaning end of discussion.

Penny took it in stride, perhaps understanding this was not her kitchen, and she was a visitor. Angela, however, kept eyeing Dorothy for any indication of what was wrong and to determine if her irritation was escalating. This wasn't the baking-and-bonding experience she'd imagined they would have. Maybe someone's apron strings had been tied a little too tight this morning.

A loud crash sounded from the other room, and Penny quickly excused herself to check on her boys. Concerned for any injuries, Angela would have followed, but this was her chance to speak to Dorothy alone.

"Before she comes back, can you tell me what's bothering you?"

"Oh, fuss, how could you tell?"

"Gee, that left-to-right hand wave you do that means leave it alone. Or the slamming of the oven door. Take your pick."

Angela heard Penny scolding her boys—gently, of course. But there was no telling how quickly she would return to the kitchen. She looked at Dorothy impatiently.

"Fine. You want to know? Alberto. That's what."

Angela inhaled sharply. *What did Papa do now?*

"He doesn't want to leave for Oregon on Monday. Do you know how much it will be to change our flights?"

Angela opened the refrigerator, pretending to look for more butter.

This is not good. Do not come between Dorothy and her grandchildren, Alberto.

"Did he say why?" she asked nonchalantly, masking her alarm.

"Did he ever. Says it's the trees. Can't leave the trees. Trouble with the trees."

Stunned, Angela abruptly turned to face Dorothy.

"What trouble? What does he know? How does he know?" she asked.

"Exactly. I've reminded him he's not the keeper, hasn't been for years now. I've become one of those—what are they? Broken records."

Angela returned to covering her rolls and allowing them to rise. She moved them to a corner of the counter where there wouldn't be a draft. Processing Dorothy's claim wasn't easy. Too many questions competed for answers.

What trouble? Did Mark know? Did he tell Papa?

If he hadn't, then why did Papa know and Mark didn't?

All questions she wanted to ask, but Dorothy wasn't the best one to answer them. She remained quiet, lost in thought.

"Sorry, dear. I shouldn't have said anything. I thought I could hide it, but kitchens are close quarters. They don't lend to keeping secrets, do they?"

Penny returned, and after a quick glance at the two of them, moved to Angela's side and asked what else she could do to help.

Caroline and Macie sprang into the kitchen.

"Mom, Macie and I have a great idea."

"What you think is a great idea might not be what Macie's mom and I do."

"Since there's no school, we can have a sleepover. Macie is practically family. I mean, she's Mark's cousin. What did you say? Once removed, or something like that? She could be my step-cousin, right? That can be a thing."

"I'm fine with that," Penny answered quickly, not giving Angela much time for a measured response.

Angela wavered. Caroline was older now, and she and Macie were becoming fast friends. Again, this was a better alternative, hanging out with a friend than how withdrawn Caroline had been.

"Only if you agree to actually sleep for enough hours during some part of the night," Angela said.

"We will. Promise," they said in unison. "Thank you so much, Mom! So tomorrow night?"

"Wait, opening weekend? I better talk to Mark."

"We can drop Macie off and pick her up too," Penny added.

"I guess that settles it," Angela said, forcing a smile since she felt compelled to agree.

"You're the best," Caroline said.

They ran off before Angela could say more. Maybe she didn't feel forced but busy in the kitchen and not enough energy to argue the finer points of her daughter's sleep needs.

❄

Dinner was lovely in a tense and halting kind of way. There were pleasant moments sandwiched in between other not-so-pleasant ones. Like the one where Mark asked someone to pass the salt, and Dorothy asked someone to pass the common sense.

Or the moment when Cathy said the stuffing was well seasoned and very moist and almost as good as it could be, if only it had raisins. Followed by the moment when Caroline informed her that there was another dish of stuffing with raisins just for her so she wouldn't complain.

Precious moments.

Penny and Gary struck up a great conversation about the differences between an anthropologist, which Gary was, and an archeologist, which Gary wasn't. As Mark was commenting on the varied flavors of the turkey seasoning, Gary could be heard explaining that he didn't care for the digging of bones and could never get comfortable being up close and personal with dirt.

To which Papa wasted no time in telling him he'd come to the wrong place.

His words were followed by the briefest moment of silence before all voices could be heard at once. Cathy defending. Gary clarifying. Mark interjecting. Papa chuckling, surely not having meant what he'd said to be taken so seriously in the first place.

Angela had taken as much as she could and felt it was the right time to clear the food and bring out the pies, but when she stood in reaction to the escalating voices, she misjudged how close she was to the table. Her body hit it with just enough force to rattle every dish and topple the glass nearest her.

Everything went into commotion, some reaching over with their napkins, others jumping up to help Angela.

Nothing like a good spill to help the cause, she thought.

An hour later, Dorothy served pie, and, not surprisingly, all were enjoying themselves. No complaints, though there were differing opinions about pumpkin-pie spices—cloves or no cloves. Also, a thorough comparison of apple pie and apple cobbler ensued. Nothing could compete with the apple pie for its position as the most traditional dessert, Gary claimed. To which Penny returned good-naturedly that he could keep the tradition and she'd take less crust and more streusel with a cobbler. Not to mention less baking time.

Once Caroline and Macie had finished their pie, they asked if they could start decorating the tree. Angela answered yes and was getting up from the table when Mark stood.

"I'll help the girls. You can get comfortable on the couch and give us directions," he said.

Angela frowned, but she knew this had been the plan. Having everyone's helping hands was as much about building a family memory as it was a way to spare Angela from too much time on her feet.

She watched as the strings of lights went around the tree, and the ornaments were placed near the top first until it was full all the way to the lower branches. Penny chaperoned her boys, who were putting shimmering snowflake ornaments on the tree and taking them off again. One of the boys kept trying to hang them on his shirt. When that didn't work, he tried hanging them on his brother's.

Dorothy supplied a thick, white ribbon to serve as the garland. It had metallic gold edges with names such as Wonderful, Counselor, and Emmanuel embossed on it. Angela admired how Dorothy rhythmically twisted the ribbon in a perfect pattern that wrapped the tree.

Mark positioned a step ladder so Caroline could place the angel on top. The white satin of the angel matched the ribbon. It looked as though it was an extension of the angel's dress and reminded Angela of the words "glories stream from heaven afar."

Once Caroline came off the step ladder, they all gazed at the tree.

"Just like that, and it's Christmastime!" Dorothy said.

"You found a good one," Mark told Caroline.

"I love it," Angela said. "The house feels better already."

This was the comfort and relaxation Angela had looked forward to as she stood in her quiet kitchen that morning. They stayed in the family room. One of Penny's boys had already fallen asleep next to her. Caroline had taken Macie to see the music studio Mark had added on to the house. Dorothy and Papa were seated in chairs near each other. Gary and Cathy were in the love seat, having what appeared to be a private conversation. Mark sat next to Angela on the couch. She snuggled close to him and put her feet up, full and content.

As far as she was concerned, she didn't need to move for the rest of the night.

CHAPTER 12

Mark stroked Angela's hand, glad she was sitting, and the busy part of the day was done. She was relaxed, which meant he could be too. The only thing that prevented him from resting completely and dozing off was Carl. He'd been quiet during dinner. Almost hadn't talked at all while they trimmed the tree. Which in and of itself wasn't a problem, but now that the chatter had slowed, Carl had questions.

"I gotta ask about the miracle trees. Is it true there's a treasure out there somewhere?"

Mark didn't answer at first because Carl had directed the question to Papa.

"Talk to him 'bout that," Papa said, pointing to Mark.

All eyes followed Papa's gesture.

"We found it," Mark said, his eyebrows raised, jaw tight.

"It is true!" Carl said as he let go of Peggy's hand and slapped his knee. He moved to the edge of his seat and fixed his wide-eyed gaze on Mark.

Mark met Angela's eyes, and she nodded to him. He shared what they'd discovered. The soil in the leather pouch, the seeds. He held up Angela's hand to show Carl the ring.

"What about the gold?"

"Excuse me?" Mark asked.

"The stash from the gold rush. From our great grandfather's cousin, or maybe his uncle—I don't know. He was a surveyor, worked the Klondike Gold Rush. Prospectors needed to stake claims. A lot of land needed surveying, I guess," Carl said.

Mark looked to Papa, expecting an expression that confirmed how Mark felt: that Carl was out of his mind! Only, he was nodding with a solemn face, and Mark had that familiar feeling he was about to find out yet one more thing Papa had kept to himself. As if growing miracle trees and having a tree-keeper's promise weren't enough secrets for one family, there had to be more?

He glanced around the room. Angela and Dorothy watched Papa with eager eyes. Gary sat alone as Cathy had gone to lie down with a "crushing headache," as she'd called it. He avoided looking at Penny or Carl, not wanting to reveal that this was the first he'd heard of any great-uncle or cousin. Buried gold, yes. Those rumors weren't new. But a plausible explanation? No.

"That's 'bout right," Papa said.

"Care to elaborate?" Mark asked after he released a breath.

"Carl already did. Your great-great-uncle made an awful lot of money in that gold rush. Never married. Died before he was fifty. Left it all to your great-great-granddaddy."

"And?" Mark asked impatiently. All eyes were on Papa. "Is it buried out there?"

Papa stood up and began to pace. He looked at Carl and nodded as if he were making up his mind about something.

"All I know is one of my great-grandmothers used to say she told stories with her sewing. She said her stitches could tell a story—one of the family, the trees, and the treasure," Papa said.

I can't believe this is the first I'm hearing of this. "What does that even mean?" Mark asked.

"Beats me," Papa said.

"It means she probably put it all in a quilt," Dorothy said.

Silence followed.

"I don't think we have any of her quilts," Papa said.

"Would they have been lost in the fire?" Angela asked.

"Suppose so," Papa said.

Mark remembered the boxes and the decorations he'd sorted.

"There was a small quilt in the box from Donna's house." He looked at Angela.

Angela looked at Dorothy.

"It's in the craft barn," she said.

Mark returned with the box. Angela stood at his side, and the others looked on as he opened it.

Pine-cone ornaments and a garland.

"Angela, where is the other box?" Mark asked.

"I took it to Goodwill," Angela said. "Why?"

Mark didn't have to look any deeper in the box. He knew these were the items to be given away and that the other box held the skirt and star. He'd left them resting right on top because he'd planned to show them to Angela. He'd planned to label that box too. Too late to do either of those things.

"Is this the Goodwill box? Did I—?"

His silence answered her question.

She sat down on the edge of the sofa. "I took the wrong box. It's as good as gone, isn't it?" she said mostly to herself.

"Don't fret," Dorothy said.

"Who's to say the quilt I saw had anything to do with the treasure," Mark said, hoping he could bring the color back to Angela's cheeks.

"What did you say it looked like?" Papa asked.

"Small, round."

"It wasn't star-shaped, was it?" Papa asked.

"Actually, there was a star-shaped hole in the middle," Mark said.

"You mean it was a tree skirt," Dorothy said.

"Yes, a tree skirt, and there was a quilted star . . ."

"For the top of the tree." Papa finished Mark's sentence as he stood and stared out the window. "What were the colors?" he asked after a moment.

"Red, white, green, and—"

"Gold," Papa stated more than asked.

"Yes, exactly. Some gold accents."

"What are you saying? She put a treasure map on the back of a tree skirt?" Penny asked.

"It wasn't uncommon for women to stitch records like family names and dates into quilts or other fabrics. A skilled seamstress could certainly stitch a map," Gary said, his comment met with a few blinking stares.

"I think I might be sick," Angela said.

"Oh, dear, do you need to lie down?" Dorothy asked.

"No, I mean it's gone. The box, the skirt—the map, whatever it is. I donated it to Goodwill. It could be anywhere by now. Getting it back now would be impossible."

"You don't know that. Shh, come now." Dorothy began patting Angela's shoulder.

"Even if it isn't a treasure map, that box had the things you wanted to keep," Angela said to Mark. "I feel terrible."

"It was an innocent mistake," Dorothy reminded her.

"I'll go to Goodwill first thing in the morning," Angela said.

"It's opening day," Mark said. "We don't have to worry about it."

"*You* don't have to worry. *I'm* the one who gave away priceless family heirlooms."

"Let's go at lunch." Mark didn't want Angela distraught over this.

He put the lid back on the box and put it in the hall closet for temporary storage, then absent-mindedly rearranged items in the closet for a reason to step away from the group's chatter. Some were consoling Angela, and others were asking Papa more questions about his great-uncle and the gold.

The gold. Of all the conversations he'd had with Papa, of all he'd taught him about the land, the trees, and the promise—he'd never once heard this story of buried gold.

Usually, Mark was skeptical of treasure rumors, and he was downright disgusted by most treasure hunters, but a true story of gold buried on his own land? He didn't know what to think.

CHAPTER 13

While most people thought of the day after Thanksgiving as Black Friday, Mark liked to think of the farm's annual opening day as Green Friday—a great day to choose a tree and start the holiday season with a symbol of everlasting life. Whatever the name for the day, he woke to all the usual concerns. Were the roads clear for customers? There hadn't been a severe storm overnight. Had he double-checked the sales lot? Did they have enough inventory? Yes, probably triple-checked. They were stocked and ready. He ran through a mental list of the names of loyal families that were sure to come. Yet he wasn't nervous about any of those things. He knew they'd work themselves out.

Only one thing, one person, claimed all of his anxious concern. Angela.

Thanksgiving, with all the food, family, and new friends, had been a long day for her, but she didn't end it satisfied. No, Mark knew she was distressed over that box of decorations. When all the guests had gone home, she kept apologizing for donating the wrong box. Mark had reassured her repeatedly with little success. She claimed she was no match for the combination of her mother's organizational genes combined with pregnancy hormones.

He planned to take her into town and track down the box. It had only been a few days since she'd donated it. He was sure they'd find the skirt and star. Maybe then she would finally relax. Angela stirred awake before Mark left.

"Are you helping Dorothy today?" he asked her.

"Yeah," Angela answered with eyes still closed. "But she said she wouldn't let me in the door until after lunch."

Mark chuckled, glad to know Angela wouldn't be able to overwork herself for a second day in a row.

"Good, let's plan to leave for town at noon."

❄

Mark found Papa inspecting the trees on the sales lot.

"Thanks for being here today," Mark said.

"Wouldn't miss it."

"You and Dorothy leave Monday, right?"

Papa didn't answer. Instead, he stepped closer to a tree.

Mark took off his hat and ran his fingers through his hair, wondering what was so interesting to him.

"Not exactly. Change of plans," Papa said.

This was the first Mark had heard of this. "Everything okay with Dorothy? Her daughter and grandkids?"

"Yep."

Finally, Papa looked up and strode to the end of the row. Mark hurried to catch up.

"She may still go yet. I told her I'm staying awhile, for the trees."

In an instant, Mark felt the dread he'd felt a time or two before. He remembered what he'd learned on his early morning walk, but he hadn't told Papa about a change coming. He hadn't told anybody.

"Why would you do that?" he asked calmly.

"Don't know yet. I expect I'll find out soon enough."

They didn't have any more time to talk about it. Carl arrived, along with a group of their seasonal employees. They all had a chance to meet, and Mark assigned them stations. Carl would supervise the baler and shaker, Papa would stay on the sales lot, and Mark would be at the cash register for at least part of the time.

On his way to the farmhouse, he saw Brett coming through the side door.

"Hey, good to see you, man. What are you doing here?"

Brett wore a wide, happy grin and held up one of Dorothy's orange rolls. "I heard you needed help cleaning up breakfast."

They shook hands, and Mark gave him a hearty slap on the back. "How's your dad?"

"Feeling good enough to give me a hard time. Told me I better come out here and check on you."

"Glad to hear it."

They stood for a minute until they spotted the first customers driving into the parking lot.

"Are you staying? Or stopping by?" Mark asked.

Brett smiled another half-grin. "Actually, my dad wants me to come home with a tree."

"Well, what do you know? Mr. Marine wants a tree."

"Yeah, it must be the new hip. He has pain, but I think he feels like he's got a second chance at life or something."

"That's great! I tell you what. You get first pick, any tree you want. I guess if you don't see one you like, you know where we keep the others," Mark joked.

"I feel kinda bad not coming to help today."

Mark grabbed him by the shoulder. "Cut it out, would you? The tree is on the house. Go on. I've got customers."

Noon came, and there were a handful of customers on the lot, but Mark could think only about making the trip into town with Angela. The farm would be fine without him for an hour or two.

The traffic was heavier than usual due to Black Friday shoppers, but that didn't bother Mark. He held Angela's hand and told her how he liked the sunlight in her hair.

"Eyes on the road, Mr. Shafer. The turn for Goodwill is right there." She pointed for emphasis. "And thank you," she said, giving him one of her flirtatious smiles, the kind that made his heart race, distracting him even more.

❄

"Yes, I know what you're talking about," the woman behind the register said. "Let me get Wynona."

"Wy, can you come on up here a sec?" she called to the back of the store. Directing her attention back to Mark and Angela, she asked if they could stand to the side.

There were no less than ten people in line behind them.

"Who knew?" Mark said, nodding to the long line. "Good thing they don't sell trees here."

"At least not fresh-cut ones," Angela said, pointing to a few artificial ones.

"How can I help ya today?" a stocky woman asked. She had straight black hair with two gray patches at her temples, kind eyes, and a hearty voice. "Name's Wynona."

"I donated some things on Monday. We're looking for a tree skirt and a star topper. They were handmade. Delicate. Have you seen them?"

"Oh yeah, couldn't miss those. 'Bout took my breath away, and I woulda bought 'em myself, but I'm moving in a week and my hubby, Ben, would notta liked me bringing home one more thing from work." She gestured to the sales floor. "You can guess I do that a lot. Tough place to work when we have so many goodies coming in."

As she said the word *goodies*, her attention shifted to the endcap of the nearest aisle, where she began rearranging an eclectic selection of purses and handbags. She moved the smaller ones to the top hooks and the larger ones to the bottom row. She held up a used drawstring bag.

"See what I mean? This here's a Dooney and Bourke. Bet you never thought you'd see a bucket bag from the eighties again, did you?"

Mark and Angela shook their heads in unison.

"Can you show us where they are? We didn't see them with the holiday items. We're happy to buy them back," Mark said.

"Can't. They're gone. Sold same day we put 'em out. Looked like they were going to a good home, though. Nice lady and her daughter. She was pleased as punch, that's what I remember."

Mark winced. Sold. In one day. Not that he was surprised. He wasn't a professional appraiser, but he'd seen them and could tell they were valuable. One glance at Angela, though, and he knew he needed to get her out of there.

"Thanks for your help." He offered quickly. He guided Angela with his hand on the small of her back. "Let's go."

In the truck, Angela was already crying. Mark knew enough not to tell her it was going to be okay.

"Sorry. I'm so sorry. I thought they'd be here, you know? I can't believe they're gone and it's my fault—your grandmother's quilt and a map to the gold."

"Hey," he said, purposely sharp. "I'm not mad. You don't have to keep apologizing. Those things had been in a box for decades. Our family didn't even know they were there. At least someone is enjoying them now." The words came quickly, though Mark worked to hide his own disappointment. "As for any gold, I don't want anything to do with it. If there really was a map on it, I think it's better for everyone if it's gone."

"You don't mean that." More tears flowed at his words.

This time he cupped her cheek with his hand and wiped away her tears with his thumb. "I do mean it," he said softly. "This is why. I can't stand anything that upsets you. I don't want anything to do with hunting for a treasure. Greed ruins people. It ruins families. I say we're better off without it."

Angela searched through her purse for tissues and regained her composure. Mark started the truck, and they drove back to the farm. Neither spoke as they passed through the town center. Once they turned onto the long road to their property, Angela turned to him.

"Do you think we'll ever know if there's gold buried somewhere on the farm?"

He sighed before answering. "I don't, but gold or not, one thing I can tell you is I'm not going to become a greedy, obsessed treasure hunter. Hard work pays better in more ways than one."

"Here's what I think," she said, no tears this time. "Maybe we'll never know. But we don't have to be overcome by greed. You know what keeps us safe from that? Keeping our love strong for each other and for our family."

She made a compelling argument. He picked up her hand and kissed it.

"Another reason I love you."

❄

They drove up to the farmhouse. Mark quickly kissed Angela and headed off to the sales lot. She took her time getting out of the truck and stretching her legs. As she walked up the porch steps, she noticed an old red Chevy stopped by the fence on the main road. Carl and Penny stood beside it. Carl was leaning into the open passenger window. Penny stood beside him with her arms folded. It was a curious sight, but what stopped Angela in her tracks was how animated Carl had become as he stood back, pointing and gesturing forcefully toward the end of the road.

Angela was already thinking about what they would eat for dinner and the ache in her feet, but as she moved toward the farmhouse, she heard the truck drive off. The truck bed looked full of equipment. What kind, she couldn't tell. She watched Carl and Penny exchange a few words and then walk their separate ways. Carl headed the same direction as Mark had a few minutes earlier, and Penny came toward the house.

Angela decided to wait for her on the porch. "Who was that?" she asked as casually as she could.

Penny appeared startled as if she had been in deep thought.

"Who? Oh, I don't know." Her voice faltered, and she turned to look at the road. "He was lost. Needed directions."

Angela nodded. That wasn't unusual. Their property was off the beaten path, and people were often looking for another way to get to town. She wouldn't have thought about it again, but the faraway look in Penny's eyes indicated something else was bothering her.

Her stomach growled. Maybe Penny was lost in thought for any number of reasons—their move, her sister's family—who knew? Angela needed something to eat and would have to check in with Penny later.

❄

Angela stood over the toaster, watching the bread when Caroline bounced into the kitchen.

"Grandma will be here to pick me up in ten minutes," Caroline declared.

"Pick you up for what?" Angela asked, feeling blindsided.

"Oh, you know, more shopping."

"No one told me. I thought she finished all the shopping for the auction."

The toast finally popped up, rather anticlimactically.

Caroline paused before answering. "She said she never knows when she might spot something for next year." She opened the refrigerator and handed the butter to her mother. "Besides, it's good bonding time for us."

Angela didn't want to admit how much those words stung. Seemed her daughter was more interested in bonding with her grandmother than she was with her. She knew she didn't need to take it personally.

This is a good thing for Caroline, she reminded herself.

She finished buttering her toast but left it on the plate.

"Do you still want me to help you redo your room when you get back?" Angela asked, appearing to take more interest in her toast than in Caroline's answer.

"Sure, but you know what Mark said. You're not allowed to overdo it."

Angela let a frown escape.

"It's no big deal, Mom. I think Grandma's here." She playfully pulled off a piece of Angela's toast and ate it, then was out of the kitchen before Angela could respond.

That's the problem, Angela thought. *It's no big deal.*

CHAPTER 14

Caroline and Macie bargained with Angela. A promise to go to bed early in exchange for permission to walk through the trees at dawn. Angela agreed, but only because she was sure the girls would stay up giggling and then be too tired to do anything in the morning but sleep.

Saturday morning came too quickly. Angela ignored Mark's early rising and willed her body to go back to sleep as fast as possible.

The side door slammed open, and running feet pounded on the wood floors. Angela sat up, startled. She looked to Mark, who, thankfully, had already thrown on his work jeans and a long-sleeved shirt.

"What on earth?" Angela exclaimed.

They could hear Caroline shouting.

"Mom! Mark! Come see."

She burst into the room with Macie not far behind her.

"Whoa, hold on there. Your mother was still sleeping."

Caroline took gulps of air. "Sorry, Mom, but we were in the north lot—the corner near the creek."

Mark moved across the room, where could he see both girls. "The northeast corner? That's almost a mile from here. What time did you wake up?"

"I don't know, but I wanted to show Macie that little waterfall. I mean, I know it's not really a waterfall, but it could be when the water level is—"

"Slow down, Caroline. What is the emergency?"

"Are you doing some sort of soil prep out there?" Caroline asked Mark.

"Not this time of year. Why?"

"I think you better come see," she said, her breathing returning to normal.

Mark looked at Angela. She held up her hands, confused. "Go ahead."

"You and Macie let me finish getting ready. I'll be out in a minute," Mark said. He closed their bedroom door as the girls retreated down the hall.

"Don't you need to go with them?" Angela asked.

"Yes, but I'd like you to come. How about we drive? That corner is near the access road. We'll get there faster."

Angela huffed as she dressed. "This is why I say no to sleepovers."

Mark chuckled. "I don't know what they think they saw, but it seems like they're enjoying themselves." He gave her shoulders a squeeze.

"I'm glad one of us can have a good attitude about this."

❄

When they got out of the truck, the girls jogged down the snow-packed road without looking back.

"It's been awhile since we've taken a walk," Mark said as he held Angela's hand. "This is my favorite time for the trees. Not sure why, but the trees feel most alive at this time of day."

Angela didn't reply at first. She concentrated on where Caroline and Macie were running and gauging how long it would take to catch up at her current speed. Mark wasn't rushed, and she took comfort in how he matched her pace. His smile was helping to ease the irritation she felt at being pulled from her warm bed.

"Careful," she said. "If you're too happy, I might think you planned this."

Those were the last words she spoke as they rounded the corner. Mark stopped, then Angela. The girls were a few steps ahead of them, and what lay just beyond was nothing either of them expected to see.

A giant hole in the ground. Freshly dug. Or maybe lots of small holes, but either way, a good portion of the land had been torn up, the soil unearthed, roots exposed.

Mark stood frozen in place, staring. Angela released a breath she didn't realize she'd been holding.

"What . . . is . . . this?" Angela asked.

"I don't—" Mark didn't finish his sentence. His hand dropped from Angela's, and he walked forward, passing the girls. Angela followed him to the edge of the hole.

Obviously, the holes were man-made. There was nothing in nature that dug up the ground like this. Also, there was more evidence than soil and dig marks. There were odd blankets with holes and grommets. A shovel had been abandoned, thrown to the side.

Angela was about to ask Mark more questions, but his hands were balled into fists. He was clenching and unclenching them. He glanced over his shoulder at Caroline and Macie, and through gritted teeth, he spat out questions.

"What time were you here?"

"I don't know. We set our alarms for 3:30 a.m., but we got dressed and used the bathroom."

Angela shot Caroline a look.

"Probably a little after four, maybe four fifteen. I know that's earlier than what you said, Mom, but we were so excited."

"Did you see anything? Anyone?" he asked. Mark's voice was tight with restraint.

"Not really."

"Well, except for some lights," Macie said.

"That's right. We were headed this way, but we saw lights that were kind of bobbing around through the trees. It was hard to tell. My flashlight isn't the strongest."

"We were singing," Macie said somewhat apologetically.

Mark's fists opened and closed.

"When we got here, it just didn't look right," Caroline added.

Angela stepped between Mark and the girls. "Why don't you two head back and wait in the truck for us." She emphasized it with eye contact.

Once the girls were out of earshot, Mark let out a few choice words. Angela placed a hand on his shoulder, but he stepped away to walk around the perimeter of the hole. She didn't take it personally. He would need a good while to cool down.

He made his way to the large gray blanket, lifted it up, and turned it over.

"What is that? Why does it have openings?"

"It must be for warming the ground," Mark said. His hands ran over the grommets. He inspected both sides and scanned the area. "My guess is they had some kind of generator out here, something blowing warm air over the spot where they wanted to . . ."

"Dig?" Angela finished.

"Yeah, and those aren't cheap." Mark looked at Angela with steely eyes. "Let's go," he said.

"Mark, what is it?"

"Whoever was here took off in a hurry," Mark explained as he quickly began folding the blanket. He grabbed the shovel and kicked at a mound of dirt.

"And?" Angela asked, not quite catching on.

"They had enough time to take the most expensive equipment before Caroline and Macie—"

"Oh!" Realization coursed through Angela.

Before Caroline and Macie discovered them.

She shivered at the thought of how close they'd come to a confrontation. Her pulse quickened, and she turned with a start. She called to Mark, but he was already making strides to the truck.

❋

Back at the farm, there wasn't a lot of time to investigate what had happened. Customers would be arriving. Brett wasn't here to manage things. But Carl would be. Suspicion shot through Mark. He'd been working with him for a week, and suddenly someone was digging up the place. He could ask him about it, or he could keep the discovery to himself and observe Carl. These warring impulses only raised Mark's blood pressure. His stomach tightened. He couldn't bear the thought of working beside a traitor. But if he was wrong, he could risk the relationship and lose the help he so desperately needed.

By the time Carl found Mark on the sales lot, there wasn't a decision to make. Macie had already told her dad everything.

Just as well, Mark thought. *I probably wouldn't have been able to keep quiet about it.*

"Macie told me what happened out there. What can I do?" Carl asked.

Mark continued his task of moving trees. He turned his back as he moved to the next one. His eyes were trained on the tree, and he walked a few steps away.

"If you want to take rows seven through ten, that would be great," Mark said evenly. He gave Carl a quick nod.

Carl paused a minute. "Okay, sure. But the hole? I can fill it in, get the ground back to level."

"That'd be nice, but it will have to wait. Customers will be arriving, and I need you to be here." Mark's voice was strained, his words clipped.

Here, where I can see you, he thought but didn't say.

Carl wore a questioning look, and Mark felt a twinge of guilt. He had no desire to falsely accuse anyone, but there were too many unanswered questions.

"I'd like Papa to see it," Mark added.

After lunch, there was a lull in the stream of customers. This was prime time for Mark to grab a bite to eat before the evening crowd arrived. He hadn't planned on inviting Carl to join him, but under the circumstances, it seemed the best thing to do.

Inside the farmhouse, Mark grabbed two turkey sandwiches from the fridge. They sat at the dining room table, out of view from the sales counter.

"You say whoever it was left their shovel?"

"At least one of them, a small one. They probably had another one."

"You said 'they.' Do you know how many?"

Mark sat back as he chewed, turning his thoughts over. He'd assumed there was more than one person, but why?

"The girls said they saw lights bobbing around. I'm guessing headlamps. I didn't ask them how many. They said it was hard to see through the trees. Judging by the size of the hole in the ground, it would have taken one person more hours than what they could get after sundown."

"They were out there as early as sundown?"

Mark inhaled a sharp breath. He looked at Carl but quickly shifted his gaze to the window on his right.

His questions are normal. Who wouldn't be asking these kinds of questions? And yet, they seemed pointed, directed at Mark and what he thought. Was Carl simply trying to figure out what Mark knew or didn't know? He didn't like the way it felt, sitting there being asked questions by a cousin who should be answering some questions of his own.

He took another bite of his sandwich and chewed slowly as if he didn't have anything else to do, as if there wasn't a question waiting to be answered.

Carl sat up straighter in his chair, studying his own sandwich before taking another bite. He avoided any eye contact with Mark. "I mean, it makes sense, right? There aren't any lights in that corner."

"Except for one near the access road," Mark stated, watching Carl for a reaction.

"Does that road take you around to—"

"North to the frontage road or south to the front entrance." Mark couldn't tell if this was new to him or not. "I don't know, by the way."

Carl looked up from his food, confused.

"I don't know what time they were out there. I'd like to think it was after sundown because how bad would that be if they were out there in broad daylight and I didn't even know it?"

"No. You're right. They had to be out there in the dark," Carl said. "What about cameras?"

"Too much acreage."

"I mean for the access road. What if you installed one or two?"

Mark was momentarily stunned, not because he hadn't thought of it first, but because the idea could support Carl's innocence. Maybe. The suspicion was wearing him out.

"We need to get back to work," Mark declared abruptly. "But I like your idea. I'll look into it."

He would've asked Brett to do it in a heartbeat. But Mark didn't think it was such a smart idea to ask the one guy he suspected of digging up his farm to install the security cameras.

CHAPTER 15

Cathy had come for lunch on Saturday—to bring lunch, that is, for Angela. It was part of her effort to ensure Angela was getting all the rest and nourishment she needed. This time, Angela hadn't argued when she'd called and offered. Her only request was that she come around 1:00 p.m. after Mark and Carl had eaten. The early, adrenaline-filled morning had left Angela feeling weak, and she was still upset over the Goodwill fiasco.

Her mother wanted to know why she looked so ragged. Angela wasn't sure if that was a step up or down from ghastly, but she didn't dare tell her what had happened overnight. That would send Cathy into a frenzy that Angela did not have the energy to manage.

While Caroline was helping Dorothy at the Craft barn, Angela opted to tell her about her other problem.

A tale of two Christmas boxes, Angela thought. *Ha! Sounds like a Hallmark movie.*

"I must not have heard Mark or somehow confused the boxes. I took the wrong one to Goodwill," she explained. Cathy seemed confused.

"Why are you upset? What could be so important in a box that had been ignored for, what, twenty years?" Cathy asked.

"We think a treasure map," Angela quickly responded.

"Why would you give away a treasure map?"

"Not helpful, Mom," Angela said.

"Who at Goodwill would know what it was, much less what to do with it?" Cathy continued.

"I didn't do it on purpose," Angela said defensively.

"Do what on purpose?" Caroline asked as she breezed through the dining room.

"Nothing, never mind." Angela attempted to drop the subject. Caroline continued to her room and returned with a bag of glue sticks.

"I don't know how they sell anything at that store in the first place," Cathy said.

"What store?" Caroline asked, this time walking by in the other direction. "Dorothy is out of these," she said as she held up the bag.

"She's talking about Goodwill." Angela answered.

"Oh, you bought something there, Grandma," Caroline said as she left through the side door.

Cathy's face blanched. "For charity."

Angela set down her fork and examined her mother for a moment. Was she really that undone by shopping in a secondhand store? Her degree of snobbishness had somehow risen to a new level. Not that Angela was surprised, just exasperated.

"When did you—"

"Caroline took me there," she said.

"Well, that was thoughtful of you, buying something for charity—at Goodwill," Angela remarked.

"I can't help it if I can recognize quality even if the owners can't. The needlework was exquisite. Very old but in lovely condition. Whoever gave it away had no idea what they were doing." She continued talking as Angela stared at her.

"Good grief, what is it?" Cathy asked.

"What kind of needlework?"

"It was a set, rather unique. A handmade tree skirt and tree topper. Gorgeous, actually. A shame the gold accents would not work with my silver theme this year. I suppose I could change back to my gold tree, but I'd gotten so, so tired of it, you understand."

Angela jumped up and grabbed her mother's shoulders. "Are you kidding me? The quilt, the star? You have them?"

"Angela, what on earth? Control yourself. Yes. Well, no. I had them. But why?"

"What do you mean you *had* them? Where are they? The skirt is the map!"

"The tree skirt is a treasure map?" Cathy asked, clearly confused.

"Yes, we think so, but we need to see it. Where is it now? You didn't have it cleaned or restored? You didn't alter it, did you?" Angela groaned.

"I told you. I've donated them to my charity auction."

Angela was momentarily speechless.

"Then you can ask for them back."

"No. Of course I can't," Cathy said.

"You have to!" Angela said, near hysterics.

"That's out of the question. One does not ask for a donation returned without a great deal of harm to one's reputation. And don't raise your voice like that. It's disquieting."

"Disquieting? Is that what this is?" Angela's volume increased. She began pacing and mumbling to herself. "I can't believe this is happening." She stopped and faced her mother. "We are talking about a map to buried treasure. I think you can put your reputation on the line for that."

"Please, calm down. This kind of excitement can't be good for the baby. I'll look into it, all right? But it's been a few days. If it's been printed in the auction preview catalog, it will be too late."

❄

After Cathy left, Angela decided to check on Dorothy in the craft barn. She knew Dorothy would have things under control, but she needed some fresh air. As Angela left the farmhouse, Caroline appeared from the far side, as if she'd been by the front porch.

"I thought you were with Dorothy?"

"I was, but I got to see grandma before she left." She walked in step with Angela for a minute before it was obvious that she couldn't contain herself.

"Guess what? You'll never guess!" Caroline said.

"If I'll never guess, you better just tell me."

"Don't you want to guess?"

"Let's see, what is it this time? Grandma is taking you to the North Pole for Christmas?"

"Not even close." Her eyes sparkled playfully, and Angela decided to be happy that Caroline was happy.

"She's having us for lunch on Saturday," Caroline said, still beaming. "In two weeks."

"When did she tell you this? How did I miss it? Did she say why?" Angela's mind raced. What was on her mother's agenda? Cathy always had an agenda.

"Do you have to have a reason?" Caroline countered.

"I don't, but your grandmother does. She doesn't throw luncheons for the fun of it. What does she want?" The last words slipped out too easily, and Angela regretted them.

"I think she wants the three of us to spend some time together and for you to be able to put your feet up."

Angela stopped walking before they entered the barn door. "Did she say that?"

"I might have told her you didn't like how much time I was spending with her on all the shopping trips. But shopping would be too tiring for you. She thought lunch was perfect because you only needed to come and sit and eat."

Oh, sweet Caroline.

"You told her that? Does she think I'm jealous? We can tell her no. The three of us do not have to spend time together for my sake." Angela's defensiveness took over. She approached the door to get inside before she said anything else she would regret.

"Please, Mom?" Caroline asked.

"No," Angela snapped.

"We've already chosen the menu, and she said I can make the cookies you like."

Angela stopped, hand on the door handle, her back still to her daughter. "She said you could cook in her kitchen or she'd have her chef bake your recipe?"

"What do you mean? Of course she'll let me cook at her place. I've told her everything I'd need to make them just the way you like—from scratch, with a mix of semisweet chips, and white ones too."

Angela slowly turned around to see her daughter's face full of hope. She was no match for those pleading eyes.

"Two weeks?"

"Yep. Saturday the thirteenth."

"Okay, then. Lunch for the three of us," Angela said, nodding her consent to Caroline. She could endure whatever motives her mother might have if it meant this much to her daughter.

"Yay! It's gonna be great. You'll see!"

Once inside the craft barn, Angela put thoughts of lunch with her mother out of her mind. She was in one of her favorite places—and could talk to one of her favorite people. Though with the steady stream of customers, she wasn't sure Dorothy would have time for conversation. They didn't need to have a lengthy one. Angela just wanted to know Dorothy's travel plans. And more importantly, how she and Papa were getting along.

"We're here to help," Angela said as they approached the back of the barn.

"Bless you!" Dorothy said. "Caroline, be a dear and find another box of our Christmas bags."

Caroline ran off before Dorothy could finish. Angela approached and reached for one of the aprons hanging on a hook behind the cash register. She attempted to put it on but didn't get very far. Dorothy was staring at her, and when Angela looked up, she noticed a few customers were as well.

They let out a collective laugh.

"That apron isn't going to fit over that baby!" Dorothy announced. "No matter. I'm not putting you to work anyway. Come sit on a stool and keep me company."

Angela might have protested if there hadn't been a line of waiting customers. She positioned herself so she could bag the items and hand them to the customers. Caroline returned just in time to provide more.

"Well done," Dorothy said. "Can you find a few more of the pine boughs? I know there are at least three more with holly berries. Bring those out and put them on the table by the front door."

Again, Caroline was on her way to the back room as Dorothy finished her instructions.

"You two couldn't have come at a better time," she said.

"About that," Angela said, hoping it sounded like a natural transition. "What did you and Papa decide to do about . . . Oregon?"

She held her breath unintentionally, feeling like she was risking the good mood in the room as well as Dorothy's focused attention.

"You mean what did *I* decide?" Dorothy asked Angela and, without missing a beat, quoted the price of goods to a customer, then finished the transaction.

The next customer stepped up, and a friendly conversation ensued between the three of them. Comments on the weather and the trees always gave way to questions about Angela's baby. When was she due, and did she know what she was having? She didn't mind answering, though she did consider customizing a T-shirt to read "Boy. Due in January. Thanks for asking."

A lull at the cash register and Caroline at the front of the craft barn provided a bit of privacy. Dorothy turned to Angela.

"I'm staying here."

Angela had a hard time figuring out if Dorothy was happy about it or not.

"I called my daughter. She understands."

"Do you feel good about it? Are you . . ." she strained to finish her question, "upset with Papa?"

"Heavens, no. He's not leaving the trees, and I'm not leaving him. Besides, my daughter isn't having a baby this year. You are!"

Angela could feel warmth in her cheeks from gratitude or relief—she wasn't sure which.

"I told my daughter I'm not leaving until your baby is born. I'll visit her next year when I can have a good, long stay."

Angela was about to thank her, possibly hug her, but Dorothy's attention was immediately given to the next customer. They chatted, and Angela wrapped a snow globe in tissue paper, then double bagged it, all the while feeling humbled by Dorothy's selflessness.

❉

Angela couldn't get ready for bed fast enough. Opening weekend was always busy, but the day had started much too early when the girls came clamoring into the house. She wanted to crawl under the covers and drift to sleep.

Mark arrived and looked as tired as she felt.

"Dorothy is staying for the holiday," she said, smiling, head on the pillow, eyes closed.

"Glad to hear it," Mark said, though most of the energy was gone from his voice.

Angela's phone rang. She sat up and answered it. One hand held the phone to her ear, the other rested over her eyes, forcing them closed. She listened and responded with "I see," and "Okay," and "I'll let him know."

She finished the call and opened her eyes. Mark was at the end of the bed.

"Let me know what?"

Angela sat up straighter and sighed.

"Cathy bought the tree skirt and topper at Goodwill," Angela informed Mark.

"That's a miracle! I mean, what are the chances? Your mother is something else!"

Angela waited until Mark paused and noticed she had more to say.

"She bought them and promptly donated them to her charity auction."

"Okay, she can *undonate* them. She understands the part about a 'precious family heirloom,' right?"

"No. She can't. She called to let me know they've already been printed in some auction preview book," Angela said.

They stared at each other for a moment.

"There's only one way to get them back," she said. Angela's stare turned into a frown, then she put her face in her hands.

"I'll do almost anything, but I'm not going to steal from a charity!" Mark said.

She tossed a pillow at him. "Not steal them. Buy them! You'll need to go to the auction and be the highest bidder."

"What if these aren't the things Papa was talking about?"

"They sound close enough. Besides, they're not some cheap manufactured pieces. These are handsewn by your great-great-grandmother," Angela said.

"Who I am sure was a very lovely woman. But I don't know. Your mother's auction is a black-tie event, Angela. Do we have any idea how much it will cost to buy them back?" Mark picked up the pillow and walked around to Angela's side.

She shook her head. "You've got this all wrong. You're forgetting something very important."

"What would that be?" Mark asked, sounding worn out.

"Aren't you the keeper of the trees?" she asked, aware they didn't talk about this often.

"Yes," he answered abruptly.

"You promised to protect the trees, right?"

"I don't see what that has to do with tree skirts and treasure hunters."

"Hear me out. I know you don't like the thought of being greedy. You want nothing to do with it," Angela started.

"Got that right."

"And the last thing you said you would ever want to be caught doing was digging for some treasure that probably didn't even exist."

"Right again."

"Let's say for argument's sake there *is* a treasure and some ill-intentioned people are after it. And they'll stop at nothing to get it, including destroying the farm or the trees. Wouldn't you, *the keeper of the trees*, be responsible to find the treasure before they do? Wouldn't protecting the treasure be part of safeguarding the land?"

Mark gripped the pillow tightly and then released it. He tossed it over to his side of the bed, then stared at Angela for a long minute. She watched his jaw tighten and then relax and the lines on his forehead disappear. He sat on the edge of the bed and leaned in. "You know how cute you are when you're all worked up about something?"

Angela grinned. "You mean when I'm right!" She patted her hands against his chest for emphasis.

"That too," he said and kissed her lips. Once, twice, then deeply.

She pulled back and inhaled. "If you are trying to distract me, it won't work."

"No tricks. I can't resist you." He kissed her forehead. "You also convinced me. I'll go to the auction and buy my grandmother's things. If anyone is going to find a pile of gold around here, it will be us. All I need now is a tuxedo."

CHAPTER 16

Get in, bid high, get out. Mark repeated the strategy to himself as if he'd suddenly taken up meditation and it was his new mantra. The week had gone by in a flash, and he'd been lucky enough to find a tuxedo to rent. He'd expected Angela to go with him, but she'd declined. Her reasons included everything from an aversion to her mother's friends to feeling the need to stay home and take it easy. On that last point, Mark agreed.

Though not attending the auction, Angela had plenty of bidding tactics. She peppered him with various what-if scenarios. She cautioned him against becoming too confrontational with a certain senator's wife.

"Let's hope she has zero interest in tree skirts or toppers," Angela said, leaving out the caution her mother had passed along that the woman was a shark or maybe a barracuda or some other horribly demeaning political name. "Just stay away from her," Angela concluded.

"You know I can't control who wants the items," Mark said. "It sounds like you are telling me to avoid everyone in the room."

"That would be fine too. Good idea."

Mark laughed. He hadn't seen Angela this serious about something in a long time—wait, scratch that—the baby's room. This auction had become baby-room serious.

"I heard they allow anonymous bidders," Mark tried to tease. "Why isn't that an option?"

"Number one, this isn't Sotheby's. Number two, if they have anonymous bidders, they would be prominent collectors. They're anonymous so they don't accidentally drive up the price. And three, from what I know, you would have to do more than register. You'd probably have to show proof of your assets."

"I see. Well, don't worry," he said. "I got this."

Mostly, he said to himself.

Get in, bid high, get out.

❋

For such a large art gallery, the room where the auction was being hosted was relatively small, its round tables arranged snugly in a horseshoe pattern around the center. He rechecked his table assignment and looked for the one marked twenty-two.

This isn't so bad. At least there's food.

He found his table and took a seat. He didn't see anyone he knew, which, of course, he hadn't expected to. Names of the women Angela told him to avoid crossed his mind—the senator's wife and another woman, a Mrs. Cortez. He scanned the faces in the room. A few couples were seated nearby, but mostly groups of women were busy greeting each other. All of them could fit the descriptions in one way or another.

Didn't matter. He wasn't here to be seen or to socialize. He was here for a star and a tree skirt.

"Who do we have here?" A woman's voice sounded behind him. Mark stood to introduce himself. He offered to shake her hand, but she only glanced at Mark's outstretched arm as she motioned to the drink in her right hand and the auction number in her left.

I get it, Mark thought. *Don't shake hands with the competition.*

"Your name is?" he asked. *She might not be willing to shake my hand, but I can at least find out her name.*

"Aren't you handsomely out of place?" she said. "Ms. Millhouse. Call me Aleesha, with a *shh* sound."

Uh, no, thank you.

"Nice to meet you, Ms. Millhouse."

He took his seat and purposefully looked in the direction of the auctioneer. Another woman approached the table, with two others close behind.

Mark endured the tiny sandwiches and endless banter about who was wearing what and who was vacationing where. Only when the auction began, and they talked about who had donated what did his ears perk up. No one would connect his Shafer name with his mother-in-law's name, but he was curious about any useful information they might have.

He wasn't surprised when they started discussing Cathy's contributions to the auction, but he shifted in his chair anyway. It wasn't a conversation he thought he should be listening to. Not that he could do anything about it now.

"I have no idea where she found the pieces. Who knew she was into antique embroidery? Usually she floods the auction with imported crystal or designer ornaments from France. Remember those? This year's donations are downright homey," one woman said.

"I heard she has another grandbaby on the way," another woman chimed in. "Maybe she's losing her touch." A ripple of polite laughter traveled around the table.

Mark maintained his posture, never allowing his eyes to stray from the front of the room. As far as he was concerned, they could pretend he wasn't there. He did feel a surge of defensiveness, though. Sure, Cathy had her faults, but who did they think they were?

The auctioneer began describing the next item: the tree skirt. Mark was confused. Shouldn't he be describing the tree topper as well? He grabbed his program and scanned the listing again. There it was, something he hadn't noticed it before. The star topper and skirt would be auctioned separately.

They're a set, he wanted to announce, but he knew better than to call attention to the items he intended to buy.

He waited for the opening bid. It was low. He was tempted to raise his number, but he waited. A woman on the other side of the room raised hers. Someone else a few tables away raised hers. The price was still reasonable. He was patient, and as the auctioneer was calling the price, he finally held up his number. He squirmed in his chair as all eyes in the room turned to him when the auctioneer said, "The gentleman at table twenty-two, number five."

The women at his table were staring the hardest.

The auctioneer continued, and Mark didn't realize he was holding his breath until the gavel sounded, and he was awarded the bid.

Well, he thought, *that wasn't so bad.*

He adjusted his posture, readying himself to bid on the star when the auctioneer declared it was time for a break. The room erupted into spontaneous chatter. Two of the ladies at his table asked him questions simultaneously.

"Are you a collector?"

"Do you have plans for the piece?"

Funny how they weren't calling it *homey* anymore. For one brief moment, he wanted to put these ladies in their place, but he still had one more piece to buy.

"I'm a collector—of trees. That tree skirt, well, it reminds me of my family. If you'll excuse me."

After collecting his claim ticket, he returned to the table as the auctioneer presented the next item: the star topper. Mark sensed the women at the table monitoring him. He sat perfectly still, practicing his unimpressed facial expression and even checking the time to prove his disinterest.

Unfortunately, Ms. Millhouse didn't take the hint. When the bidding started, she immediately raised her number, and Mark couldn't stop himself in time. He glanced at her in disbelief, and she winked at him. Winked!

Mark knew he shouldn't bid, at least not right away, so he held back. A string of bidders raised their numbers, the price going up like a geyser. He masked his annoyance with another glance at the time. Ms. Millhouse—Alee-shha—bid again. Mark didn't look at her this time. Instead, he calmly raised his number, garnering the auctioneer's attention and half the room again.

He ignored the whispers at his table and kept raising his number. Ms. Millhouse kept raising hers.

No more eye contact, he told himself.

His strategy worked. Starved of any reaction from Mark, Ms. Millhouse stopped bidding.

The star was seconds away from his ownership when the auctioneer announced an anonymous bidder had placed a bid.

So much for controlling his reaction. His chair jerked backward as he attempted to stand up, but he caught himself. How infuriating! The star was almost his, and now the price had jumped. He didn't even know who he was competing against, but given what Angela had said about anonymous bidders, he knew this might be trouble.

He raised his number again. This generated more whispers at his table. Another bid, this time much higher. Mark swallowed at the sum as wild thoughts ran through his mind. This was outrageous.

Was this Cathy? Was she trying to make up for donating the pieces in the first place?

Did someone else know about the buried treasure and what this star meant?

Buried treasure. Mark looked around the room and instantly felt foolish. Did he really think there was anything buried on his tree farm and that this quilted star was going to lead him to it?

Was he about to pay $2,500 for it?

How had he become a fool? The kind of treasure-hunting fool he vowed he'd never be?

The auctioneer's voice called one last time, and Ms. Millhouse raised her number and called a much higher amount. This time Mark looked at her, and she nodded graciously.

She's bidding for me, Mark realized. *Oh, no she's not.* He wanted no part of being indebted to her.

He raised his number, calling an ever-so-slightly higher bid, and just as quickly saw a sour expression replace the kinder one on her face. He sat back in his chair, relieved.

He'd buy his own family heirloom, thank you very much.

The anonymous bidder doubled the bid. Mark nearly choked. For a handmade star made of fabric and ribbon?

His shock and racing thoughts delayed his reaction just long enough for the gavel to hit and the star to be given to the unknown bidder.

The rest of the auction was a blur for Mark. In the end, he paid for and picked up the tree skirt, but he couldn't even look at it. He put it under his arm, and on his way out, Ms. Millhouse purposely strode past him.

"Pity about the matching star," she said, her voice dripping with sarcasm and spite. "I would have been open to a joint-custody agreement."

❄

Mark replayed the auction in his mind on the drive home from Providence. Even if he hadn't been momentarily stunned, he wouldn't have paid $8,000 for a handmade star, would he?

When he got home, he didn't expect Angela to be waiting by the door.

"What is it? Are you okay?" he asked.

She gave him a stop-asking-me-that glare.

"It feels like you've been gone forever. How did it go?" she asked, searching his empty hands.

"Are you looking for this?" He pulled the tree skirt out from under his overcoat.

"You got them! Let's see." She took the skirt out of his hand, moved across the room, and had it unfolded on the dining room table in seconds.

"Oh, it's gorgeous."

He approached her side and studied it with her. There it was—stitches to match the outline of their property. Lines for the road to the east and the one that ran north—or was it the other way around? He gently rotated it a half turn. The embroidery was delicate but only as precise as a decades-old, hand-stitched map could be.

"It looks like this part of the map is mostly the land. The cabin must be on the star—somewhere here in the center." Angela pointed to the empty space created by the star-shaped edge, where the skirt would normally tie around the base of the tree.

"Must be," Mark mumbled.

"Where is it?" Angela asked.

"What?"

"Cut it out. The star. Let's put them together."

He inhaled sharply and avoided her eyes. "Can't," he said and turned away.

"What do you mean?"

He turned back around and met Angela's bewildered gaze. "I didn't get it. There was another bidder, an anonymous one."

It took Angela a moment. She shook her head. "Are you saying you don't have it?"

"That's what I'm saying."

"Why didn't you bid higher?" The exasperation in Angela's voice bordered on desperation.

"We don't have that kind of money, that's why."

"Well, maybe we do, but we'll never know because we don't have the rest of the map," Angela said.

"We can't spend it before we have it," Mark argued.

"Why not? That's what everyone else does. It's practically the American way," Angela said, pushing the chair into the dining table for emphasis.

Mark reached for her and drew her close to him. "It's not our way. Look, I'm frustrated too."

She leaned into the hug and then suddenly stepped back to the table.

"So that's it? No way to find the treasure?"

Mark sighed. "Even if we had the star, it's been a lot of years. Over eighty. Don't you think someone would have found it by now? My dad found the box and the leather pouch. If there was more, he would have discovered it, I'm sure."

"We don't know that," Angela said, growing agitated. "Any idea who the bidder could be?"

"Do you know anyone named anonymous?" he said, staring at the tree skirt.

"You don't think it was my mom, do you?" Angela asked.

"I did for a minute. But the event organizers would know it was her. I don't think she would risk it."

"Yeah, you're right. Then who?"

"A Christmas collector? Someone into antique holiday Americana or who has a thing for stars? I don't know," Mark said.

"Is there any way it could have been—never mind. I don't want to ask it," Angela said.

"Carl? I've already thought it." Mark let out a full breath. "He was here and heard it all, but could he have that kind of money?"

"Maybe from the sale of their farm?"

Mark hadn't considered that. "But his parents are still living and retired."

Angela nodded and used both hands to pull her hair behind her neck. She twisted and wrapped it around as she stared at the tree skirt with Mark.

"Hey, you didn't get your hopes up, did you?" Mark asked.

Angela released her hair and waved one of her arms. "No. It's not that."

"Then what is it?"

"I don't know what to call it. I feel like . . . no, it's dumb."

"Tell me."

"I feel like it's out there and can only be found at the right—"

"Time?" Mark finished her sentence.

"And only by the right person," Angela said.

They looked at each other and back at the tree skirt.

"As long as that person isn't anonymous, I'm okay with that," Mark said.

CHAPTER 17

Mark dealt with losing the bid for the tree topper the way he dealt with all his frustrations—he worked long and hard, outside. Fresh air and the friendly faces of customers reminded him of what mattered most. He also had something to look forward to—the celebration he was planning for Angela.

He had everything in place. Angela's mother had whisked her away to the spa. One advantage of a mother-in-law eager to spoil her daughter—all Mark had to do was ask, and Cathy had agreed. With Angela out of the house, Dorothy had decorated their bedroom in tropical colors, including a change of their bedding and new towels. Mark had chosen some of it but deferred to Dorothy when it came to color schemes and thread count. She'd even gotten room dividers and had them fitted with beach scenes. In the corner was a little table dressed for a tropical-island dinner. He pulled his favorite framed wedding photo from the bottom of his dresser and added it to the center of their table. Standing on the wintry porch of the farmhouse, Angela glowed in the winter sun.

Mark chuckled at the room, hoping that if Angela didn't absolutely love it, she would get a good laugh. At the very least, she would never forget the pink-flamingo curtains and pineapple-shaped pillows. He placed an anniversary card with three chocolate truffles on her nightstand. If he'd learned anything in the last few years, it was the power of chocolate to soothe a woman's soul.

Seeing the finished room, Mark's confidence surged. Angela would be pampered all day, come home to the surprise of a decorated bedroom, and then have a cozy dinner at home.

He and Carl had a few more things to finish before they could wrap up for the day, so he sent Angela a text.

Working late. Rest when you get home. Dinner ready soon.

They had to haul more trees to restock the sales lot. Mark couldn't complain about the work when sales were strong, even if it meant it would take them a little longer to finish.

If he'd planned to take Angela to a restaurant, he wouldn't have dared work late and keep her waiting. But this was different. Hopefully, she was in a relaxed mood from all the spa treatments her mother had likely insisted on. She'd be able to see their newly decorated bedroom and know they didn't have a long drive before they could eat.

He appreciated Carl's help more than ever. Carl hadn't complained either. Outside of Papa and Brett, the man could work like no other. He couldn't have asked for a better employee—someone who instinctively knew when to step in and what to do.

They quickly moved the trees, Carl having no trouble setting them up and spacing them appropriately. Despite their efficient process, the sun had long since disappeared below the horizon, and Mark could feel the temperature dropping. Angela wouldn't mind a short wait, but this was pushing it.

They only had four more trees to stage. He stopped to send her another quick text.

Be there soon. Carl and I are almost done. Have you seen the bedroom?

Carl took notice of Mark's pause. "Hey, you can go. No need for both of us to be out here," Carl said.

"The work goes faster with both of us. I don't mind."

Angela's reply came back. *Couldn't miss it. Love it and love you. Take your time. My feet are up, and I'm reading.*

Perfect, he thought as he put his phone back in his pocket. Before he could grab the next tree, his phone rang. He answered, expecting it to be Angela. It was Papa.

That's odd. Sure, Dorothy had bought him a cell phone, but he vowed to never use it unless it was . . . an emergency.

"Hello," Mark answered quickly.

True to his word, Papa said he saw a truck on the access road. "I'm not as close as you. Better get over there as quick as you can."

As soon as Mark ended the call, he looked at Carl. He hesitated for a minute but chose to set aside his suspicions.

"We've got to leave these trees," he said. "Come with me. We need to go help Papa."

They hopped in Mark's truck and took the access road to the northeast corner of the farm. The old gate they had fixed up to block access was open. As Mark drove past it, he could see it had been dented, probably by a truck.

"Pretty brazen," Mark mumbled.

"Is your papa out here?" Carl asked with obvious worry.

"No, he's a little to the west, in the fifth-year lot. It has some elevation and a clear view of the road." Mark paused before continuing. "I have to ask. Do you have any idea who could be out here?" Or who has been digging up the place?"

Mark had barely finished his question when the truck's headlights illuminated two men.

"Would you look at that! Two of them." Mark's mind raced with what to do next.

"One for each of us. I'll take the tall one," Carl said.

A few hundred yards from their parked truck, the men were clad in black, wore headlamps, and carried equipment. Mark hit the gas to block their truck with his. As he sped across the uneven pavement, his tires spit rocks and broken asphalt. He angled his headlights in their direction.

The men dropped their equipment and ran.

Carl jumped out of the truck as Mark was throwing it into park. Carl sprinted after them, though he didn't have any light. Neither did Mark. There was probably a flashlight in his glove compartment or toolbox, but the men already had a head start. Mark took off running after the shorter of the two men. His high school track days were long behind him, and this guy, even with his short legs, had enough lead time to be out of reach.

But Mark kept pursuit. He was dodging trees and following the man's erratic pattern until the man pulled off his headlamp. He threw it to his left and ran to the right. Mark followed but quickly lost the ability to see his target.

He heard shouting and spun around to check on Carl. Though it was only seconds, by the time he turned back, there was no sign of the man he'd been chasing. Concerned about what was happening with Carl, he began running in the direction of the shouting.

As he ran, Mark could see the outline of the two men fist-fighting. He wouldn't have been able to tell who was who except for the headlamp worn by one of the men. Mark's adrenaline spiked at the sight of the man throwing punches at Carl—his headlamp had to have been blinding him as well. Mark didn't feel his legs, only the burning in his lungs, as he ran. He watched as Carl ripped the headlamp off the man's head. Within seconds, it was hard for Mark to recognize either of them.

He arrived in time to seize the man and prevent him from throwing another punch.

Only he'd grabbed Carl instead.

The other man, momentarily confused, backed up and took off running, soon enshrouded by the trees and thick darkness. Mark realized what he'd done, but not soon enough to undo it. Though Carl had fought his way out of Mark's grip, they both stared in the direction the man had run, accepting reality—he'd gotten away.

Mark turned to look closely at Carl. The man's face was a bloodied mess. Anger swelled in Mark. They hadn't caught either man, one of them had badly beaten Carl, and he still didn't have any answers.

Who were they, and how did they know about the gold?

"I almost had him," Carl said as he patted his top lip with the back of his hand.

"Sorry. My fault. Without the headlamp, I couldn't tell you apart."

"Let's get their equipment and then get you cleaned up."

They retreated back to the access road, gathering the shovels and generator as they went. When they reached the two parked trucks, Mark loaded what he was carrying into the back, but Carl went straight to the other truck.

Mark pulled out his phone to call 911 but stopped when he saw Carl under the hood.

"If they come back, they aren't taking this home," Carl said to Mark as he approached.

"Good point. Here, let me help you with that."

"I've got a wrench. Just need some light."

After removing the mounting brackets and disconnecting the battery, Carl lifted it out and handed it to Mark.

"There," Carl said, slamming the hood down. "No one's going anywhere in this truck tonight."

CHAPTER 18

Angela checked her phone again. It had been an hour since Mark's last text, and he wasn't responding to her messages. She was coping better than usual, knowing they would be eating in. The day at the spa was helping too. A gentle massage had released much of the tension in her neck, and she was glad to have a full range of motion again. She hadn't been aware of how tight her muscles had become, but they were still relaxed now. She had that spa-induced, "it's-all-good" attitude.

Besides, it was hard to be annoyed resting on a bed with new tropical sheets, complete with decorations Mark obviously went to a lot of trouble to find. She saw truffles and a card on the nightstand. She ate one while holding the card but decided to wait until Mark was there before she opened it. Sighing, she rubbed the side of her belly. Mark was always surprising and looking out for her. Even under extra stress, he'd managed a room make-over. Curling up with her pillow and filled with gratitude for Mark, she was more tired than she realized. She had no memory of falling asleep—only of waking up alone.

Groggy and disoriented, she checked her phone. Another hour had passed and still no word from Mark. Her breathing quickened, and her heart pounded. Working late was one thing, but for Mark to miss dinner with no explanation or text meant something was wrong.

She turned on the lights and began changing out of her comfy clothes into jeans and a sweater—both maternity sized and also comfy but better for braving the cold.

She tried to keep her thoughts from racing.

Crossing the room, she saw the pink-flamingo curtains and remembered the whole reason she was expecting him home for dinner in the first place.

What could be more important than our anniversary? She fumed to herself.

A battle between worry and indignation ensued.

How dare he?

Maybe he's hurt.

Did he forget that he *planned this date?*

If he's not in the hospital, he better have a good explanation.

Mark wasn't prone to injury, but her imagination could offer up some pretty gruesome farm-related accidents. The worry was winning, and she had to keep telling herself something must have come up, and Mark would be walking through the door any minute.

She sat down in the corner chair, slowed her breathing, and called his cell. It went right to voicemail. She tried Papa's phone and got the same result.

She left the room to find anyone who might know anything about what was going on. As she neared the end of the hall, Mark and Carl burst through the side door by the living room.

"Come on, you sit down while I call the police," Mark said to Carl.

Angela stared in disbelief. Carl's face was a mess. She examined Mark and couldn't see any sign of injury, but—oh, was he angry.

"You don't have to do that, Mark," Carl said quietly, nursing his swollen lip.

"Digging up the land is wrong, but assaulting one of my employees—that's going too far," Mark nearly shouted.

Angela rushed to Carl's side. "How bad is it? What do you need? Let me get you some ice."

On her way to the kitchen, she encountered Mark.

"Mark, what happened? Are you okay?"

He grabbed her and hugged her fiercely. Too fiercely.

"I'm sorry about tonight. I'll explain later. I've got to—"

Angela pushed against his tightening arms to get a better look at him. "I'm fine. It doesn't even matter. I need to know you're okay."

He released her as brusquely as he'd hugged her.

"I'll make it up to you," he said, still gripping her shoulders.

She shook her head. He still hadn't answered the question, but given that she couldn't see any blood or bruises, she decided he was fine—for now. Angela grabbed an ice pack from the freezer for Carl.

"Don't call the police on my account," Carl said again, this time standing up and moving toward the door.

"Hey, where are you going?" Mark asked.

"Penny. She's got to be worried sick by now. I've got to get home to her."

Mark approached him, phone in hand. "The police are gonna need you to make a statement."

A flash of anger crossed Carl's face. His jaw tightened, and he said more emphatically, "I'm not talking to the police. I'm not making a report or pressing charges. I'll be back to help you, but I'm going home to Penny."

Angela could see the war of confusion and fury on Mark's face. He slammed his phone down on the table.

"Maybe take a few days off, then. Come back when you aren't black and blue."

After the door closed, Angela didn't know which way to move—toward Mark or away from him. Did he need to talk or time to cool down?

Before she could decide, Papa entered the side door.

"Saw Carl leaving. Did you find anyone on the access road?" he asked.

Mark glanced at Angela before answering. "We almost had them." He breathed out a slow, controlled breath.

"Who? Almost had who?" Angela asked as she puzzled over Mark's reaction.

"They'll be back," Papa said. "Treasure hunters don't quit."

Mark nodded. "If not for the treasure, they'll come back for their truck and generator."

"They left in a hurry again, did they?"

Angela was grateful Papa had come when he did. Mark was visibly calmer.

❄

Good thing she'd had that nap as it turned out to be quite a long night. The police officer left after taking down all the details from

Mark. Not that there were many. Mark's descriptions of the two men were vague. They were of average height and had been dressed in black, and were in good physical condition. He'd been almost face-to-face with the man who'd punched Carl, but it had been too dark, and Mark didn't recall any distinguishing features.

The truck was a good lead. It had been reported stolen a few weeks earlier. They would send a tow truck to impound it in the morning.

By the time Angela and Mark returned to their bedroom, they were both exhausted.

"If nothing else, I'm glad you arranged for Caroline to stay with my mom tonight. She's already worried about the trees. This would have upset her."

Mark nodded. "I tried to think of everything," he said as he glanced around the room.

Angela felt a wave of gratitude, followed by empathy and a mix of attraction and, sadly, fatigue. "The spa day was pretty nice, and I love what you did with the place."

"I told you I'd make it up to you."

"You didn't have to," Angela said.

"It was everything I'd planned except actual time together," Mark pointed out. "The one thing you tell me you want more of."

Angela smiled in agreement. "True, but—"

"How about Christmas Eve?"

"What about it?"

"Christmas Eve. The farm will be closed. After Caroline goes to sleep, the house will be quiet, the presents ready."

Angela was already settling into bed, pulling the covers up to her chin. "The night before Christmas, huh?" she said as she closed her eyes. "I'm imagining it. Go on."

"I'll have this little table set up again, and it will just be you and me and whatever you want—music, dessert—you name it, you'll have it."

"Hmm. I like it. Sounds like a date," she said.

"Good."

"Mark?"

"What is it?" he asked.

"Come to bed," she said.

CHAPTER 19

"I'm glad you're here," Mark said, putting his arm on Papa's shoulder. "Is this why you didn't go to Oregon. Did you know something like this was going to happen?".

Papa stayed focused on the hole in the ground as he rocked back on his heels.

"Can't say I did. Never imagined this kind of damage."

"What do you make of it?" Mark asked.

"Desperation," Papa said solemnly.

"I know treasure hunters become desperate. You've mentioned that before. But I've been thinking. You said my dad would randomly dig all over the place, right?"

"Seemed so."

"These guys keep coming back to this corner of the farm—at great risk because we're keeping a close watch."

"Not close enough if they're getting through."

Mark sighed. "Right, the gate didn't hold up and the cameras failed to record anything. Probably should have read the user's manual. Short of camping out here, I'm not sure what else—"

"I can be your night guard," Papa declared.

Mark scratched his head. This wasn't going the way he'd imagined. No doubt Papa could have held his own in his younger years, but now that he was over eighty, he didn't have any business being a security guard, much less at night.

"That's not why I asked you to come see this, not what I wanted to ask you. What is it about this part of the farm? Why would someone have reason to believe the treasure is here?" Mark finally spelled it out.

Papa walked around the hole in the ground. "Where are the shovels?" Papa asked.

"What shovels? You mean the ones I have in the back of the truck?"

"Best go get 'em," Papa ordered. "Let's get to it. The hole won't fill itself," he said with a tone that meant, "Don't argue."

Mark wondered if Papa was purposely ignoring his question or if he hadn't heard it. New questions came to Mark's mind.

What didn't Papa want to talk about?

"Don't just stand there. Use that shovel in your hand. Let's get this ground level again."

Mark stepped up to the mound of dirt and hefted as much as he could. They alternated in a lock-step rhythm, one on each end of the hole, evenly distributing the displaced soil. The only sound between them was their breathing and the scraping of metal on dirt. Mark had all but forgotten he had asked a question when Papa started talking in sentences punctuated by his shoveling.

"This corner of the land had a second homestead, least a start o' one."

Mark paused in his motion, but only for a moment. Something *else* he didn't know.

"Why a second?"

"Brothers William and Henry were to inherit this land. Share it fifty-fifty."

More soil thrown in the hole.

"Is that right?"

"From what my daddy told me, this corner here almost had a house and barn, and another lot for sales."

"Why would they do that?" Mark asked, tossing soil in after Papa.

"Don't know, but I can guess they weren't the best of friends, those two."

Mark rested on his shovel handle. "Yeah, if Henry married William's girlfriend, I'm surprised William would even let them set foot here."

Papa focused on the dirt, lifting and dumping.

"My daddy said Henry showed up one day asking for his half of the farm, said he wanted to live on it and run it. William agreed to opposite corners and different tree varieties. See, William was happy to put the past where it belonged—behind them."

"Then why didn't they build a house?" Mark asked as he resumed shoveling.

"Turned out Henry didn't want the land. He'd heard about their cousin dying, leaving William a mountain of gold."

At that, Mark stopped shoveling again, though Papa didn't even look up.

"You left this part out of the story on Thanksgiving Day."

"You know how I feel about treasure hunters," Papa barked back, breaking his even tone.

"Ah. You think Carl could have done this? Do we have any proof?"

"Who said anything about proof? All I know is what my daddy said about William and Henry. As soon as Henry heard that William came into some money, he pretended to want his half of the land, even though he'd abandoned it some five years earlier. Didn't take William long to figure it out."

"What did he do? Pay him? William bought Henry's half of the land?"

"Yes, he did," Papa said.

"With gold?"

"So the story goes."

The mound of dirt was disappearing, the hole near full.

"But why would anyone think there was gold buried here?" Mark took a panoramic view of the trees, thinking again about how many acres stretched out around them.

"Probably 'cause William buried the rest of it."

Mark stared at Papa, speechless.

"Don't look at me like that. My daddy said Henry wouldn't leave them alone. Returned six months later asking for more. Then he started breaking into the house to steal it. William decided it was better for everybody for the gold to be in a safe hiding place."

"So he buried it? Somewhere on this land?" Mark had resisted any and every rumor of buried treasure he'd ever heard about the farm, but this was different. This wasn't a rumor—it was family history. Papa had no reason to invent this story. He was simply reporting what his father had told him. And why would his father make up any of it?

"Do we know any more about Henry's side of the story? Why didn't he spend it?"

"Can't say. Just that my daddy felt the way his daddy felt, and so on. Greed does to families what fire does to trees. Devours them whole. Our treasure *is* the trees. We take care of them and they take care of us. As for gold, well, hearts wind up broken when they've been set too much on it."

The hole was filled, the soil mounded. Maybe not as compacted as it had been before it was dug up and displaced, but it was good enough. Mark stared at it, wondering if they had just buried a large stash of gold coins. He wanted nothing to do with greed, and yet, for the first time, he believed there might be something valuable underground. A new feeling arose in him—the desire to find it.

CHAPTER 20

Angela should have known better. From the moment Caroline had announced they were invited to a "lunch," Angela should have investigated and found out what her mother was up to. But Caroline had been so happy, so hopeful that Angela chose to leave it alone.

When her mother appeared at her door on Friday with a new maternity sweater dress, claiming she couldn't leave the store without it and wouldn't Angela love to wear it to lunch tomorrow? Yeah, that should've been a big red flag. When she insisted Caroline go home with her to spend the night so they could bake cookies in the morning, Angela ought to have demanded an explanation for what those two were really cooking up.

But she hadn't done that. Instead, she accepted the dress and allowed Caroline to pack her overnight bag and walk out of the farmhouse with a hug and a "see you tomorrow."

Even when Cathy had said, "Eleven forty-five. Don't be late," Angela had simply replied, "Don't worry, I won't."

All this in an effort to stay calm for her baby boy. The closer she got to her due date, the more she wanted to be centered, grounded, and able to handle whatever life had in store.

She took one deep breath and knocked. The door didn't open right away.

Strange.

She checked her phone. 11:44.

Ha. I'm even one minute early.

She closed her eyes and took another deep breath, all while congratulating herself on remaining neutral. *Totally centered.*

The door opened. Angela opened her eyes, but Walters was not standing there.

"Surprise!"

Once she got over the initial shock of fifty women shouting at her, Angela found her way inside her mother's house and sank into a chair. She'd been bracing for lunch with her mother and whatever agenda she might have had, not for a lunch where she was the center of attention.

In her mother's defense, they *were* having lunch. The buffet table proved the point. It was covered with enough appetizers, salads, and desserts to feed twice as many women than were present. Angela was assaulted by the competing aromas of Greek salad skewers and chicken-avocado wraps. The cheesecake-stuffed strawberries looked the most appealing, but then again, so did the mini blue petit fours with tiny bow ties. She usually dealt with buffet indecisiveness by having a little bit of everything. Doing that at her mother's buffet table would mean definite heartburn.

Before she could spend too much time choosing what to put on her plate, her mother's guests greeted her and engaged her in small talk. Soon, she spotted someone her age. It took a moment for the woman to recognize her, but thankfully she did. Sydney and Angela had bonded over comparative political and economic systems in high school. Their fathers were both politicians, after all.

They talked long enough for Angela to learn Sydney was currently a journalist who had worked for several publications and was considering a move to D.C. Angela shared how much she loved the tree farm.

"I never would have sought out farm life, but now I wouldn't give it up," she said.

"There you are," a familiar voice called.

Angela turned to see a woman moving through the crowd toward her.

"Look at you. Aren't you the cutest pregnant lady! How do you do it? Are you getting weekly facials? Are you on a low-inflammatory diet? It can't all be pregnancy hormones. You look so good!"

This was Ashley, the friend from high school who had taken over Angela's apartment-manager job and who usually couldn't ask fewer than three questions per breath. But they'd kept in touch the last few years, and instead of lamenting their differences, Angela had come to appreciate Ashley's friendship.

"Thanks, but no special diet. No facials. I'm telling you, it's farm life. How's John?"

"You know—working on his next deal. But he's good and good to me. That's what counts, right? Did I tell you where he took me for my birthday? Wait, did I tell you where we went for Labor Day? Hold on. Never mind all of that. When are you going to give me a tour of your mother's mansion?"

Angela nearly choked on her lemonade. "First, let's not call it that, and second, she'll have a fit if I leave the group."

Ashely didn't have time to be disappointed as one of Cathy's friends complimented her shoes. Angela could see she was about to make a new friend.

Dorothy came over and gave her arm a slight squeeze. "Did we give you a fright?" she asked.

"You knew about this and didn't tell me!"

"What? You'd have me on your mother's bad side?"

"Fair point," Angela conceded.

"Besides, you should know your daughter instigated it. She begged your mother. Cathy kept telling her you loathed parties, especially at her house."

Angela cringed inwardly. She was right, but it did sound terrible to hear it out loud.

"Caroline can be hard to turn down," Angela said.

"Especially for a grandmother." Dorothy shook her head. "So you'll not hold it against your mum?"

Every now and then, Dorothy's accent came through a little stronger, softening Angela every time.

"No, I don't think I will," Angela said, feeling more gratitude than grief over her mother's surprise.

Angela had opened the generous and numerous gifts and was fighting back tears. Not from stress but from gratitude for the overwhelming kindness. She didn't feel like she could say thank you enough.

"Goodness, I almost forgot!" Cathy announced and jumped up from her chair.

No one was quite sure what she up to. Some women remained seated, chatting. Others came and hugged Angela goodbye, wishing her well. She thought it might be a good time to excuse herself to the restroom given all the lemonade she'd been drinking.

She bypassed the one in the hallway for the guests. Though it meant climbing the stairs, she used the bathroom nearest her childhood bedroom. It afforded her a moment of quiet. She didn't linger too long at the sink—a glance at her reflection showed teary eyes. When she stepped out, she couldn't resist opening the door to her room. It had been years.

To her surprise, it wasn't exactly how she'd left it. It was partially remodeled, with half the room holding the furniture she had as a teenager, the other half sporting new paint, and what appeared to be guest furniture. She didn't mind in the least that her room was different; quite the opposite—it wasn't her room. Hadn't been for years. What surprised her was the incompleteness of the remodel. She'd never known her mother to rest until a room was finished. Yet here was her bedroom in disarray.

She walked in and pulled the nightstand drawer open. A little blue journal rested inside. Angela gasped. *Could it be?*

Her hand reached for it, opening it to the ribbon bookmark. *Cathy grounded me tonight.*

Angela laughed at a common entry and at her younger self always referring to her mother as Cathy. She was about to close the book but decided to keep reading the entry.

Or at least she said she would check her calendar and inform me when it was convenient for her to have me grounded. I swear I will never be friends with that woman. She doesn't understand me, and I don't want to understand her. One day I'll live as far away as I can and

The writing ended midsentence.

Angela collapsed onto the edge of her bed. She covered her mouth with her hand.

And what?

She didn't have to ask. Her teenage anger and pain returned. The memory of wanting to put as much distance between her and her mother came readily enough. Only here, sitting in her room and reading those words after spending several hours on the receiving end of her mother's generosity, she felt great regret. Tears streamed down her face as she sat weeping for the relationship she'd missed out on with her mother. The baby boy she was carrying kicked once. Then came the flurry of kicks that always made her laugh. She rubbed her abdomen and thought about the kind of mother she was, the kind of mother she wanted to be. No one got a perfect mother, she realized. While not exactly an earth-shattering insight, it shifted her thoughts and gave her a new resolve to make the best of the relationship she and her mother did have.

At that, she remembered where she was and the house full of people, possibly wondering where she was. She closed the journal, put it back in her nightstand drawer, and left the room.

She emerged downstairs to see that a good number of guests had left and her mother standing at the door waving.

"There you are. I have one more gift for you. You must open it, and I promised to take a picture as you do."

Angela didn't know what that meant, but she sat in the chair by all the gifts, and her mother handed her a soft, square package. The paper was white and tied with a flat blue ribbon. A little plain but also elegant. She looked to her mother, who was holding her camera.

"Who is this from?" she asked.

"I couldn't fly her over for this," Cathy said.

"Florinda?" Angela stared down at the gift, wanting but not wanting to open it.

"Don't be scared of it."

Once she slid off the ribbon and removed the tape, the paper fell away to reveal a blanket. It was a lovely shade of baby blue with satin edges, and there in the middle was an embroidered white lamb.

Several women let out sighs, but Angela looked to Caroline and then Dorothy and then her mother.

Meu cordeirinho. My little lamb.

Cathy snapped a few pictures and disappeared, explaining she wanted to send them as soon as possible. Dorothy, Caroline, and the others admired the blanket and said their goodbyes.

Cathy, not Walters or any of the staff, helped Angela pack up the truck with the gifts. It was evident there were more gifts than available space. Caroline volunteered to stay at her grandmother's house another night and make more room for the presents.

Angela straightened up and put both hands on her lower back. She was about to say no, but before she could, her mother chimed in.

"Only if it's okay with your mother," she said without any strain.

For the first time maybe ever, Cathy hadn't interrupted, preempted, or overridden Angela.

Caroline waited with expectant eyes. Cathy continued arranging packages.

"Is it, Mom? Is it okay with you?" Caroline asked.

Angela's mind raced with the implications of her mother's simple statement. No judgment, no imperative. She was deferring to Angela.

"You know what? Yes, it's fine with me," Angela said. She finally felt free to say yes. No more uneasiness over how much time her mother and Caroline were spending together, no longer threatened by Cathy's efforts—only the realization that they were close and that she had nothing to fear.

"Did you pack enough things?" Cathy asked.

"Yep, I wasn't sure what I wanted to wear today—so I packed extra outfits just in case," Caroline answered.

It wasn't often Angela went looking for Mark on the sales lot, but she didn't know where else he could be. The tow company was here for the truck and needed a signature. He wasn't answering his phone, and she figured the fresh air would do her some good. Besides, she enjoyed the rows of trees and the memory of her first time at the Shafer farm.

Well, that first night she may not have been able to savor the moment, with Papa's talk of miracle trees and his insistence that they believe in them. But she had come to remember that night with much fondness. She never thought she'd be living there and married to the owner, but here she was, ready to have his baby. Yes, that first night had changed her life. It still brought a smile to her face.

Of course, she'd be smiling a little more if she could find Mark, but she was three rows in, and she still didn't see him. At the end of the fourth, she paused to check her phone to see if he'd replied. He hadn't. She studied the trees to her right and left. A couple with two children came around the corner. She greeted them and moved out of their way by backing into the tree behind her.

She heard a man's voice.

"That's why you're here," it said.

"No. I told you, no," another man said in a low but angry voice.

"You say that like you have a choice. You're in this too. It won't take much for them to figure it out."

Angela glanced around. No one was taking immediate notice of her, and though she felt awkward standing so close to a tree for no reason, she couldn't move. She didn't enjoy eavesdropping—truthfully, she preferred to mind her own business—but she heard something familiar and urgent in the voices. She couldn't help herself.

"That's enough. You need to go. Now."

"All you have to do is borrow it. What's the harm in borrowing a little Christmas cheer?"

Angela's back straightened. What Christmas cheer? That could mean any number of things. Decorations? Were two men conspiring to steal Christmas crafts?

She imagined the two men raiding Donna's barn—one grabbing North Pole signs and snow globes, the other loading up on stuffed snowmen and jars of orange marmalade. *Unlikely.*

Another couple strolled down the row in her direction. She pretended to scrutinize the tree branches she was crowding while trying to keep the lower limbs from poking her round belly.

A tree! They must be talking about stealing a tree. She kept listening but, at the same time, replayed their words for other clues. She didn't dare move her head, though she desperately wanted to try and get a look at the pair.

"If you make more trouble, I'm picking up the phone and making that call."

Angela heard some rude remarks and a final threat.

"Go ahead. You do what you have to do, and so will I."

She instinctively stepped out to the middle of the path and put her hands in her pockets. Why she felt conspicuous, she didn't know, but the last thing she wanted was for anyone to see her, especially these two men.

In her panic, she turned one way, then the other, toward the very end of the row where she could turn back toward the farmhouse, only to collide with Mark.

"There you are," he said. "I've been looking for you."

"Me? I've been looking for you," Angela insisted.

"Where have you been?" Mark asked.

"Right here," Angela answered honestly, but then Mark gave her a questioning look.

"I was . . . this tree . . ." Angela felt a rush of heat flood her cheeks as she recalled the conversation she'd overheard. She stepped around Mark, looking frantically for who could have been in the other row.

"Are you sure you're feeling okay?"

"I am fine!" She spun around, tired of always having to declare her fine-ness. "Did you see anyone in the next row over?" She heard a squeal of tires from the parking lot and looked in time to see a small, silver Toyota.

"No. Why? Is there a problem?" he asked.

Angela studied the parking lot but could see only families walking in and out. "Hopefully not," she answered distantly and then remembered why she'd been looking for Mark in the first place.

"The tow company is here for the truck. Did they find you?" she asked.

"Yeah. Taken care of."

As he answered, they both turned to the sound of the tow truck lumbering down the side road with a red Chevy pickup, front end high like a seesaw board.

Where have I seen that truck? she wondered.

Mark reached for her arm, guiding her as they walked. "Let's go inside."

Angela continued searching the lot and the trees. Soon they were at the side door, and before they could open it, Carl stumbled out. He moved out of the way to let them by, but his eyes were downcast.

"Everything okay?"

"Hey, Mark. Hi, Angela. Yeah . . . no. I was . . . looking for my keys. Not sure what I did with them." He gave a half-smile and walked away, clearly not interested in a conversation.

Mark held the door for Angela, but her feet didn't move. She stood staring off in the distance as it all clicked.

The familiar voice was Carl's. The Chevy was the one he'd been leaning into last week!

"Are we going in?" Mark asked her gently, still holding the door.

Angela shook her head but walked through the door, sending Mark conflicting messages.

"We need to talk," she said.

"You need to rest," he said.

"Fine. I'll rest if you come with me and listen."

He followed her past the fireplace and the sales counter, across the dining room, and beyond their music room. By the time they reached their bedroom, Angela couldn't keep it in.

"I was wrong about Carl," she announced.

CHAPTER 21

"Hey, shh. Keep your voice down." Mark closed the door. "What do you mean?"

He didn't need to ask. She was still talking.

"I'm sorry, Mark, I really am, but I think you were right. I mean, I believe in seeing the good and giving people the benefit of the doubt and that we have to trust family, but you were right."

"Slow down. Can you fill me in?"

"It's Carl. He was with the man from the truck. I saw them after our trip to Goodwill. Penny said he was lost. Then today, just now, I heard Carl talking to someone. It had to be the man from the truck again, and the things I heard them say! Oh, Mark, I'm so sorry I didn't believe you before."

Mark listened as Angela's words gained speed, and it looked as though she might cry. He wanted her to rest on the bed or even sit down in the chair, but he was afraid the suggestion would bring tears.

"Okay, okay. Let me see if I'm getting all this. Carl has been talking to a guy who owns a truck?" He said the words slowly to see if he'd missed anything.

"Not *a* truck. The same truck the police towed out of here. I don't think the man needed directions like Penny said he did. They must know each other. The other man said Carl was 'in it too,' so maybe that means they are in on it together."

Mark paced by the end of their bed, scratching his head, avoiding eye contact. Neither one of them had gotten a good night's rest.

"Are you listening to me?" she asked.

He approached her, offering a hug. That seemed to slow her breathing.

"Why don't you tell me what they were talking about. Let's start there."

Angela took a few deep breaths. "They were arguing. Carl told him no, but I don't know why. The man said something about Carl being 'in it too' and how it wouldn't take much for 'them to figure it out.' *Them* must mean us, right?"

"What else did they say?" Mark pressed.

"I guess Carl asked him to go, but the man said all he needed to do was 'borrow a little Christmas cheer.' Carl said if he made trouble, he would make a call. But then the man threatened him. He said, 'If you don't do it, I will.'"

As Mark listened to this calmer, more coherent version of events, a mental picture began to form, a picture of Carl's reluctance to do what the other man had asked. But if what Angela heard was correct, he was still very much connected to this other man and what he was planning.

They needed more information, and the only one who could give that to him was Carl.

Mark dropped into the rocking chair in the corner of their room. He held his head in his hands, his fingers rubbing his temples. Even though Carl had shown up at the same time as the dread in Mark's chest and asked about buried treasure, it didn't prove he was digging up the farm. What Mark had witnessed Carl doing was hard, nonstop work. He'd stepped in and taken Brett's place. Carl had even been the one to finish lunch every day and say, "Let's get back at it."

Mark had all but forgotten about his original suspicions.

Until now. Until Angela was sure she'd overheard him arguing.

Mark didn't want to believe it. How could he have missed it? He'd felt all that dread the day Carl showed up at the farm. The same man who had been working by Mark's side day-in and day-out had been working against him? He didn't want to believe it, but Angela had seen him talking to the man in the truck twice. If Mark had only confronted Carl sooner, it might not have come to this. The same man attempting to find and steal buried treasure from the farm was the same man Carl knew or had some connection to. Mark couldn't let it go on any longer.

If it were just Carl, it wouldn't be difficult, but what would it do to Angela and Penny, not to mention Caroline and Macie? They had become fast friends, and more than that, they all felt like family. Frustration surged through Mark. He couldn't imagine Carl's wife and daughter being involved, but it had been one of the reasons Mark hadn't confronted Carl earlier.

Trouble was, they didn't know enough, and when Mark thought about asking Carl who the man in the red Chevy was, he lost his nerve. If Carl was guilty of something, of anything, he would need to leave. If he was innocent, there was nothing to worry about, but Mark didn't want to lose one of the best workers on his farm to a false accusation.

They couldn't prove Carl was the anonymous buyer at the auction, but who else could it be? They had grilled poor Cathy until she was nearly in tears, insisting she had not been the buyer. No, it had to be Carl. He had been there when they'd talked about the tree skirt and star. He'd heard what Papa said it could mean. Mark hated to think it, but it had to be Carl.

❄

Carl arrived sporting his signature cheerful smile, his lips no longer swollen, but his eye bruised and chin a little purple. Mark resisted any feelings of empathy. No wonder Carl hadn't wanted to talk to the police. He hadn't been assaulted by a trespasser—he'd been putting on a good show with his partner. The thought boiled Mark's blood. Instead of a soft start-up, he chose to get right to the point.

"You no longer work here," Mark told his cousin. "We know what you've been up to, and it has to stop."

He could see the shock on Carl's face, but he didn't let that stop him.

"Let me explain," Carl said.

"It's too late for that."

"It's not what you think," Carl said more earnestly.

"Pretty sure it is, and that's what every guilty party says. I just want to know where you got the money to buy the star."

Carl rocked back on his heels. "You think *I* went and bought it? I swear it wasn't me. You've gotta believe me."

"No, I don't." Mark remained calm. "The only thing I have to do is make sure you understand you aren't welcome here anymore. Not you or your family." Mark immediately regretted those last words.

"Seriously? You think my wife had anything to do with this? Listen to yourself. Can you even believe what you're saying?" Carl challenged, though Mark could see he looked far more sad than angry.

"We're not pressing charges. If you go quietly and don't come back, we'll forget we even met, so long as you forget about any treasure on this land."

Carl attempted to speak but hung his head in silence instead. He held up his hands and retreated toward the door. "If that's the way you want it," he said and turned his back.

Mark released all the air from his lungs. He watched the door and waited a minute to be sure Carl was gone, and this nightmare could be over. The quiet house settled around him. He moved to the bay window, stared out at the trees, and vowed to do better by them. He couldn't shake how dejected Carl had looked, how he hadn't fought back. He hadn't put up a fight like Mark expected a treasure hunter would, especially when he was cut off from finding his long-sought-after prize.

What difference does it make? Mark argued with himself. There was too much evidence pointing toward some kind of involvement.

One week to the holiday and it was only going to get busier. All Mark could do was hope Carl would stay away. That, and look into hiring a security firm. And be the first to find the gold Papa said was buried on their land. This would be a different kind of Christmas.

❄

Mark couldn't sleep, and the last thing he wanted to do was disturb Angela. He used his best stealth maneuvers for getting out of bed and slipped out of the room. He didn't regret asking Carl to leave, but he couldn't stop thinking how sad his cousin had seemed.

Maybe he'd done some theater. He was a good actor, that was all.

He wandered into the kitchen and turned on the small light over the sink, then eyed the microwave popcorn on the pantry shelf. Too loud. He looked for the ice cream, then remembered Angela had recently taken a liking to it. Cookies and milk on a covered plate were just the fix. Lucky for him, Caroline hadn't skimped when baking those cookies for the surprise shower.

The wind howled outside the window. The temperature was dropping. By morning it would be ten below. His thoughts turned to the ground-warming equipment he still had. Perhaps it was the midnight-snack effect, but a new idea formed. He jammed the last cookie into his mouth and brushed off his hands.

There, in the front room, Angela had allowed Caroline to put the tree skirt under the tree. Only a few presents rested on top of it. He cleared them off and gently brought the skirt into the kitchen, not wanting to turn on the bright dining-room light. He turned it over and scanned the underside. He studied the edges, but his attention was drawn to the star-shaped opening in the center. He began to see the land clearly, understand the orientation better. Based on the markings for the creek and the north-facing elevated ridge, the area of land represented by that empty star was not very large.

Tree branches scratched at a dark window in the front room. The wind continued howling. He turned and adjusted the quilt until finally, it struck him.

The east point had to be where the cabin was. The west point of the missing star had to be the location of the barn. Which meant the north point—the longest of the points—was the toolshed. The old root cellar.

Of all the places, he thought. *Could it be?*

"Mark?" Angela's whisper sounded from the other side of the kitchen. "What are you doing?"

Startled, he stood up and folded the tree skirt, then unfolded it.

"Grabbed a snack. Couldn't sleep. Sorry, did I wake you? I tried to be quiet."

"No. I think it was the wind," she said.

He stood staring at her, deciding. Should he put the skirt back or tell her about his discovery?

Well, it's more like a theory, he reasoned. *Just a guess.*

He shut off the lights and walked back to their bedroom with her, keeping the tree skirt tucked under his arm.

CHAPTER 22

Morning found Mark energetic despite losing more than a few hours of sleep. He dressed for what he knew would be some of the coldest temperatures of the year. Thankfully, Brett was returning to work, which would allow Mark some time to investigate the toolshed.

It hadn't changed much in the last few years. Papa had said if he got to gardening again, he'd use it for what it was intended, storing vegetables, instead of a resting place for their old equipment. But Papa had always found odd jobs to do at the farm, and planting a vegetable garden wasn't one of them. They hadn't even filled in the hole in the wall where they'd found his dad's hidden box. They had long since kept it in a safe.

Mark was drawn to the wall. He pulled a broken board away from the edge of the hiding place his dad had made. He'd been clever to put the box there. It had gone undetected for years. He couldn't stand there staring at it without thinking of the Christmas Day he and Angela had discovered the box, the moment he'd put the ring on her finger, or the first time they'd shared a kiss. As happy as the memory was, he couldn't keep standing there. He had work to do.

Picturing his father hiding the box in the wall reminded him of the stories he'd heard about all the holes his father had dug. Mark had always thought his dad had chosen to put the box in the toolshed because it was more accessible and less likely to be harmed than if he buried it elsewhere. Could it be his dad had another reason? Did his dad know what Mark had figured out at midnight? Did the back of the tree topper indicate there was more treasure somewhere near this toolshed?

Mark's attention shifted from the hole in the wall to the entire wall, which formed the north side of the old root cellar. He felt it with his gloved hands, his breath creating a fog around him as his heart pounded.

This could be it, he thought calmly at first. Then excitement coursed through him. "This could really be it," he said out loud.

He grabbed a shovel from the assorted tools in the corner and started expanding the existing hole. Before long, he thought better of the dirt piling up at his feet and found a bucket. Though only a five-gallon one, it would have to do. He'd have to work more slowly, but maybe that was best. Mark needed to be careful of the cellar's structural integrity built into the hilly ridge so long ago. Slower digging with pauses to take the soil outside of the cellar was a safer strategy.

Ten bucket loads, or fifty gallons of dirt later, Mark stopped to examine his work. The initial rush of adrenaline had worn off. He let the shovel rest on the ground and stood back a step to see what he'd done.

Where there had been a small, square shelf-like hole in the wall, a full-sized hollow spanned floor to ceiling. Deep enough for him to step into if he wanted. But his goal wasn't to give the cellar a new floor plan—it was to uncover what it was hiding.

So far, he'd only uncovered more dirt.

Fueled by frustration instead of excitement, he attacked the back of the hollow with fervor.

It has to be here, he insisted. He reviewed the evidence, his father's box, and the tree-skirt map. He stopped shoveling, momentarily doubting those tenuous clues, but then thrust the shovel into the dirt wall with renewed energy.

It's here. It has to be.

❄

Long after lunch, Brett found him sitting outside the cellar entrance next to a fair-sized mound of dirt.

"What do we have here?" he asked. "You excavating? Need topsoil this time of year?"

Mark shook his head and rubbed his forehead with the side of his arm. He contemplated telling Brett what he was up to but couldn't bring himself to admit it, at least not directly.

"Making more room in there."

"For what? Did you break that much equipment while I was gone?"

"Not quite." Mark stood and stretched his shoulders and back. "How is the sales lot?"

"Busy. But that's not why I'm here. The mayor and his family are here. They are asking for you."

Mark stood and brushed off the sides of his jeans. "Forgot that was today."

"You know, all you need to do is ask, and I can help you with the toolshed. No reason for it to be a one-man job," Brett offered.

"Thanks. Appreciate it. You are helping me, though. If you weren't here, I wouldn't be able to get this sorted out."

Brett gave him a sideways look. "You sure you don't want to talk about it?"

"Talk about what?"

"I heard about the hole-digging and the men who got away. I heard you asked Carl to leave. I'm sorry, Mark. Maybe it wouldn't have gone down that way had I been here."

"Nothing he did is your fault. We both know you needed to be with your dad."

Neither spoke as they approached the farmhouse. Mark could see customers filling the sales lot. What had he been thinking? He didn't have time to dig holes! Anger swelled in him. He'd vowed to never hunt treasure, to never lose sight of what was important. Yet here he was, all because he thought he could imagine the rest of an eighty-year-old handmade treasure map.

"Mark, you okay?"

"Fine," he quipped.

"Is it true?" Brett asked.

Mark questioned him with his expression.

"Coins from a gold rush? Buried here somewhere?"

"Maybe. Maybe not. I don't think we'll ever know."

The mayor and his wife were on the porch, posing for some selfies with their daughters and grandchildren. As Mark approached, he noticed their matching outfits and bright smiles and became aware of how dirty he was. Normally, he was comfortable as the less-than-fashionable tree farmer, but standing there coated in a layer of dirt only provided more evidence of how consumed he'd been.

"How bad do I look?" Mark asked, discreetly brushing off his sleeves.

Brett was staring at the mayor and his family.

"Do I have time to change and come back before they're done?" Mark asked, a little more insistent.

Brett shrugged. "I don't know."

Mark tracked Brett's line of sight. It was fixed on the mayor's daughter—the single one.

"You haven't heard a word I said."

"What was that?" Brett finally made eye contact with Mark.

"Do I have time to run and change my clothes?"

"I don't think so. The mayor is waving to you," Brett said.

Mark quickly waved back. The mayor broke ranks with his family and shook their hands. They discussed one of the town's upcoming park projects, and then the mayor questioned Mark about a tree-planting campaign for Arbor Day. "I can catch up with you after your busy season," the mayor finished.

"Glad to help any way I can," Mark said. "I'll be looking forward to it."

"Arbor Day—that's a good holiday right there," Brett said.

Mark and the mayor looked at him for a moment before Mark responded. "Brett is my most trusted farm manager. There isn't anything he can't do around here. I'll have him put some ideas together for a tree-planting project."

"Sounds good to me. Thank you, Mark. Good to meet you, Brett."

He excused himself and returned to his family.

Mark leaned over to Brett. "It's probably now or never."

Brett gave Mark a sheepish grin and stepped forward. He offered to take pictures of the family. They readily agreed, and Brett snapped a couple pictures, then called out, "Smile like you mean it."

"Okay, smile at the mayor."

The family all turned to a surprised mayor.

"Now, everyone, smile at the real boss."

No one knew quite who he meant, but they looked at each other—some with smiles and some with bewildered expressions.

Their son-in-law looked to his wife, who was looking at their three-year-old. One of the daughters looked at their mom, and within seconds they were breaking out in laughter, including the mayor. Brett captured it all in a series of snapshots.

They thanked him, and as he went to return the camera, the mayor's daughter reached for it.

"Impressive. You got my dad to break character," she said. "Are you a photographer?"

"Just having fun."

"Well, thanks," she said, pausing before she turned back toward her family.

Mark watched as Brett hesitated.

"Let me know how the pictures turn out," he called to her.

Not the worst thing he could say, Mark thought.

She turned back to face him again. "Sure. How about I send you one? What's your number? My name's Julie, by the way. Nice farm you have here."

Mark waited until Julie and her family retreated to the parking lot before congratulating Brett.

"For what?" he asked.

"She asked for your number," Mark pointed out.

"Yeah. I guess she did, didn't she?" Brett said.

"She also likes the farm," Mark said. "I wouldn't let her get away."

❆

Mark was glad he hadn't told Angela about his discovery. No, not discovery. More like a wild guess.

A cookie-fueled midnight imagining—that's all it was, he chided himself. At least he hadn't needlessly gotten her hopes up and embarrassed himself in the process.

He walked through the side door, where Angela stopped him.

"Don't take another step," she said. "I don't know where you've been or what you've been doing, but I haven't spent the week cleaning just to see a layer of dirt on everything."

Another frustration. He couldn't even walk through his own home.

"What do you suggest?" he asked, choosing a playful tone to mask his irritation. "Use the porch as a changing room?"

"No, but that's not a bad idea. Come around to the back door. I'll meet you there."

He followed her instructions, and when she opened the door, she held up an empty laundry basket. "Take off as much as you can without scaring anyone who might be able to see you. Here are some things I grabbed."

"Is this necessary? It's not like I work in an office. We live on a farm—dirt is a staple. Also, it's cold!"

"Do you want to mop floors tonight?"

Mark held back a chuckle. What was it about pregnancy? He understood nesting, but he didn't remember Angela quite so obsessed with cleaning. He couldn't argue with her, though. The combination of her adorable pregnant shape and that intense focus in her eyes commanded all his respect.

"What were you doing anyway? You and Papa already filled the hole on the northeast corner, right?"

Mark avoided the question, pulling off his coat and then his shirt. He made eyes at Angela.

"Don't be ridiculous," she teased and went inside.

※

Mark thought he'd gotten out of explaining himself. They had climbed into bed, settled in, and said good night.

Then Angela's groggy voice pulled him from falling fully asleep. "I can tell when you're keeping secrets."

"What are you talking about?" he asked, genuinely confused.

"You don't want me to know you went hunting today."

Mark remained silent, though he became much more awake.

She continued. "I don't care if you go looking for gold. I don't even care about the dirt. Well, I guess I do. But what hurts is when you keep things from me."

All of Mark's defenses left him. He'd been ready to explain and deflect and defend. But hearing that he might have done anything to hurt her crushed him.

He moved close enough to wrap his arm around her shoulder and whisper in her ear as lovingly as he knew how. "I'm sorry. I didn't mean to hurt you. I won't do it again."

She didn't reply. Mark could tell she was breathing slowly, deeply. *Did she fall asleep that fast?*

Another moment passed, then two. He moved back to his side of the bed.

I'll tell her again tomorrow, he decided.
"Hey, Mark?" she asked in a sleep-filled voice.
"Yeah?"
"Did you find it?"
He sighed. "No."
"That's too bad," she said. "Don't worry. You will."
In the dark, Mark smiled at her sweetness.

CHAPTER 23

Angela wasn't prepared for her mother to greet her so early on a Monday morning. At least she'd already pulled herself out of bed, gotten dressed, and had breakfast with Caroline before seeing her off to school. She couldn't claim she looked perky, but, at the very least, she wasn't ghastly.

With all that had been going on at the farm, she'd forgotten that her mother had offered to deliver several of the shower gifts Angela wasn't able to bring home on Saturday. She carried in a swing and then went back for a prepackaged assortment of bath soap, toys, and towels. Cathy announced she had one more gift and returned with a cradle. Angela didn't remember that from the shower. At all. She looked it over and then to her mother for an explanation.

"For heaven's sake, Angela, don't look at me like that," her mother said while lifting the white, wooden cradle and marching toward the baby's room.

"What did you do? I told you we have everything we need."

Her mother made a sharp turn from the baby's room to Angela's bedroom, gently pushing open the door with her shoulder. Angela quickly caught up to her.

"I didn't think you had one of these. I see I was right." Cathy stopped and examined both nightstands, then proceeded to the one with a lamp, a book, and a glass of water.

"This is a bedside cradle," she said. "Which you will thank me for before your son is even two weeks old."

Angela watched her mother position the cradle, moving it toward the bed and then a little farther away, finally deciding on a resting place. She put her hands on her hips and gave a nod.

Any resistance Angela may have had fled at the smile Cathy wore. The cradle fit perfectly. It had heart-shaped cutouts on each end that seemed quite unlike her mother's taste, and yet she was so obviously pleased with it.

"See how it rocks? Very smooth," Cathy asked and answered her own question as she reached out and tapped it into motion.

She was also pleased with herself, no doubt, but Angela detected something else. Anticipation? Giddiness? Whatever it was, it chased away any complaint or protest of Angela's. She felt tears well up in her eyes, but not from sadness or frustration. They weren't from feeling overwhelmed, either. These were happy tears—honest-to-goodness tears of gratitude for her mother's thoughtfulness.

"I don't need to wait two weeks. Thank you, Mom," she told her. "I already appreciate it. I know your grandson will too."

"Good. Does this mean you'll use it?" Cathy asked, perhaps missing the gratitude.

"Yes, I'll use it," she said. Though she was unsure she'd be able to sleep with the baby that close, because her mother had gone to the trouble, she would give it a try.

They both walked out of the bedroom and into the hall.

"Now, what about the baby's room?"

"What about it?" she asked more defensively than she should have.

"Have you already gotten all the gifts from Saturday set up and put away?"

Angela purposely walked past the baby's room and toward the front of the house. If she and her mother set foot in that nursery, it would become a boxing match. She'd want to rearrange it all and probably discover more items in need of purchase. Angela appreciated what her mother had done, but she didn't have to get in the ring with her.

"That's something Caroline and I planned to do when she got home from school today."

Angela made a mental note—*go through the shower gifts with Caroline.*

"I see," Cathy said. "I meet with the caterers again today. Are you sure we can't have you over for Christmas Eve?"

"Thanks, but we're all set. We're planning a quiet night here."

"You're looking a little pale." Her mother looked her over, head to toe, with a quizzical expression.

Angela braced herself. What would she say today? Dreadful? Ghostly?

"What is it?" Angela asked.

Her mother shook her head and walked to the door.

"Out with it."

Cathy turned and studied her again. "Good thing I brought the cradle."

Angela blinked. "What do you mean?"

"You're having this baby early," Cathy stated.

There it was. Angela was all too familiar with her mother's go-to response. Since Angela hadn't accepted her help with the nursery and had turned down the Christmas Eve dinner invite, her mother was targeting Angela's number-one fear.

"No. No, I'm not," she said defiantly.

"Don't be silly. I know my own daughter. Besides, you came early."

"Yes, but I am not you. This baby is not me. He's staying put until January 17."

"Didn't Caroline come before her due date too, now that I think of it?"

Oh, Angela wished she hadn't asked that. Her mother could dredge up painful memories with just one question. Cathy had conveniently disowned Angela after she'd married Todd and later wanted nothing to do with her first and only grandchild.

Angela stepped in front of her and opened the door. "She was two days early. Two days."

"This is your second baby, and it's a boy, and you should be prepared for anything."

"Thanks for coming by." Angela was inching closer to her mother, who was backing out the door. "We'll see you Christmas Day."

"Unless you'd like, I could come over on—"

Angela interrupted her. "Christmas Day."

That will be soon enough.

The door closed, and Angela rested against the back of it. "That was your grandmother," she said, aiming her words at her belly as she rubbed the side of it. "If that doesn't scare you into staying put, I don't know what will."

❄

When Caroline sauntered through the door, Angela wasn't sure how interested she would be in helping her set up the baby's room. Ever since Carl had stopped working at the farm, she and Macie were not spending time together.

"Grandma stopped by today. Do you want to see what she brought?"

Before she had a chance to ask for help with the room, Caroline surprised her.

"Can we finish sorting the clothes?"

"Sure."

"Then can I set up the swing? I bet I can figure it out," Caroline said.

"I bet you can," Angela replied, encouraged by her daughter's cheerful attitude.

They worked side by side until the gift bags were emptied, folded, and stored in a drawer, and the swing was tucked nicely in the corner.

"Now, all we need is the baby," Caroline joked as she gently pushed the swing.

"Oh, don't say that," Angela said too quickly.

"Why not? We're totally ready!"

"Your grandmother tried to tell me I was having him early," Angela said.

"Could you? I mean, would you?"

Angela laughed at her daughter's wide eyes. "First of all, remember what I told you? My body has a mind of its own right now. This baby will come when he's ready."

She studied Caroline's face. "Does this mean you wouldn't mind if he came early?"

"Mind? Are you kidding? I can't wait. I told Mark he'd better pick me up from school on the way to the hospital."

Caroline's excitement brought relief in waves. Angela laughed and sat in the rocking chair.

"All this time I thought you weren't happy about a brother."

"Uh, yeah, a sister would have been way better, but then I got over it. I mean, a baby is a baby—boy or girl. Besides, I'm still the older sister—boy or girl."

"You're not worried about you and me and time together?" Angela gently asked, checking her daughter's face for a reaction.

She scrunched up her nose. "Are you gonna let me hold him?"

"Yes."

"Then we're fine."

With that, she reached over, hugged Angela, and strolled out of the room.

"I'm starving," she said, calling from the hallway.

Angela surveyed the organized room. Newborn outfits hung in the closet, stacked diapers crammed the changing table, and the crib waited patiently.

She's right. Now all we need is a baby.

❄

"I heard about what happened at the auction. Too bad, really. I can only imagine how lovely the star would have been knowing what the skirt looks like," Dorothy said. "Do you have any idea who bought it?"

"None," Angela answered. "Mother denies it. I believe her. Not that she wouldn't keep something from me, but if she bought it, she'd make it known."

"I hope you don't mind. I brought you an early present."

Angela could see something wrapped in white tissue paper. "You didn't have to do this," she said.

"Isn't that the Christmas spirit? Giving because we want to, not because we have to? Here, tell me what you think."

Angela accepted it and peeled back the layers of tissue paper to reveal a star-shaped tree topper. She gasped.

"Dorothy how did you—where did this come from?" she asked with wide eyes.

"Don't get too excited. It's not what you think. I was worried I might confuse you. Turn it over."

Angela immediately flipped it over. The back was solid yellow. No gold stitches and nothing to indicate a map. She felt silly for being disappointed.

"I wasn't trying for a duplicate, you see. I came across it in town and thought it was such a shame that you didn't have the match to your tree skirt. Though I see you have an angel on top of your tree, so you may not want this. Perhaps I've made it worse."

"No, not worse at all. It was very thoughtful of you. The colors on the front, the points of the star—I just thought for a minute it could have been . . ."

Angela had no idea where the tears came from. They were thoroughly unwarranted, and the last thing she wanted was for Dorothy to see them, but in Dorothy's own words, she was far too keen to miss something like tears.

"I've gone and done it now. Forgive me. I'll take it right back. You'll never see it again."

When Dorothy reached for it, Angela gripped it tighter and smiled. "Not so fast. I'm keeping it."

"Not if it makes you cry, you're not."

"I'm still frustrated that I gave away the wrong box."

"Hand it over."

"I'll be fine. These tears are nothing. Trust me."

Dorothy gave her a suspicious look. "You're sure?"

"Positive." Angela crossed the room and set the star by the tree. She would have Mark change it out later.

"I suppose you need to have that baby and maybe your tears won't trouble you as much."

"I'm in no rush for that. Like I told my mother today, this is a January baby."

"Mmm."

"What?" Angela asked.

"Why were you telling her that?"

"Because she gave me some look and said I was having him early. Like she would know," Angela said.

"Wouldn't she?"

"Not you too!" Angela said. "No, she wouldn't! She only saw me once when I was pregnant with Caroline."

"Fine, then. January it is," Dorothy said. "Are she and Gary still coming for Christmas dinner? You didn't call that off, did you?"

"They will be here. You and Papa will too, right?"

"Wouldn't miss it."

CHAPTER 24

At Papa's suggestion, they kept the sales lot open till noon on Christmas Eve. True, they wouldn't have many customers, but that wasn't the purpose. Papa claimed Brett had been asking for the hours. Mark suspected he had another motive.

When he asked Papa if they needed a cashier on duty, he sported a sly grin and said, "No, don't think we will."

No cashier was needed. Mark couldn't argue. They didn't do it every year, and they didn't advertise, but when they could, they did. Anyone who showed up the day before Christmas went home with a tree and a smile—no wallet necessary.

Though he and Angela hadn't talked about it, Mark hadn't forgotten his promise for the night. He'd ordered the Aloha Paradise Cheesecake he hoped she'd like and staged some of the decorations. When Angela had taken Caroline to Donna's barn to wrap presents in private, Mark set up the small table in their bedroom, complete with their silver wedding-gift candlesticks.

He glanced around the room, satisfied until the memory of his last attempt at this romantic night flashed through his mind. There had been no sign of Carl and no sightings of his partners—whoever they were. But it had only been a week. The land had been left alone, but how long would they stay away? All he needed was for him and

Angela to have a quiet anniversary celebration without anyone digging up the ground. Was that too much to ask?

Angela and Caroline returned from Donna's barn with Dorothy. It was time for the sales lot to close so they could all have some lunch.

Mark gave Angela a quick hug before he headed out to help Papa and Brett secure the lot. He couldn't believe his eyes as he rounded the corner. Carl and Penny were approaching Papa. Mark's steps quickened with his heartbeat.

On Christmas Eve. Really?

He took some breaths and scanned the trees and parking lot. He couldn't see any other customers, but regardless, he didn't want a confrontation. He just wanted them to leave.

By the time he joined them on the sales lot, they'd been talking to Papa for a few minutes.

"Let's have Dorothy make a little extra. Carl and Penny will be joining us for lunch," Papa said to Mark.

Mark didn't answer, his jaw tightening as he reeled with confusion.

What was Papa talking about? Did he not remember Mark clearly stating that they would not be welcomed back? Or the part about not setting foot on the farm or he would press charges? He was too stunned to speak. As he turned his back to them and looked over at the farmhouse, he heard Penny's voice.

"We have something for you." There was a pause. "And Carl wants to explain."

He faced them, ready to push back, but Penny's voice was soft. She was holding what appeared to be a gift. There wasn't anything he needed or wanted from them, and they had to know that no present could make up for the grief and damage they'd caused. As for the explanation, he didn't think there was anything Carl could say for himself. Yet Penny looked at him with pleading eyes, and Carl's face flickered between sadness and hope.

"It's one of the coldest days of the year. Let's get inside and sort this out," Mark said, not knowing where the words came from.

If Mark had been surprised, Angela was all the more shocked when they came through the door. Caroline jumped up and hugged Macie. Angela and Penny hugged too. Mark felt like he'd missed a memo. He was about to ask for an explanation, but he didn't have to.

Carl spoke first. "Can we sit? Maybe by the tree?"

They moved to the front room and sat in pairs—Angela and Mark, Papa and Dorothy, Caroline and Macie. Brett was at the cash register, but Mark insisted he come over too.

"I knew I couldn't undo the damage that had been done, but I still felt like I needed to do what I could to make it right." He paused, straightened up on the edge of the sofa, and looked directly at Mark before he continued. "I know the man who was looking for buried treasure on your farm."

I knew it! Mark thought, ready to say it out loud except for what came next.

"He's my brother."

Penny reached over and took Carl's hand, keeping her eyes focused on him. Mark looked to Angela for a moment, then back to Carl. He'd suspected Carl was involved, but not related to the man digging up the place.

"I'm sorry I couldn't stop him. Believe me when I tell you I didn't know the lengths he'd go to. But I've put an end to it, and he won't be able to bother you again."

The fire crackled in the otherwise silent room. No one spoke, though there were more unanswered questions.

"How can you be sure?" Mark asked plainly.

"He's been out on parole. I made a call and reported everything—the trespassing and property damage. The truck was stolen too. He and his friend are both back behind bars." His voice caught in his throat, and he looked to Penny. "I'd hoped this time would be different, but I knew he'd keep trying to find the treasure until he either found it or got caught."

Mark was tempted to doubt him, to ask for proof. How did he know it wasn't some story and that this man was who he said he was? But as Carl talked, something within Mark's heart softened, and all his instincts agreed—he was hearing the truth.

"My brother had gambling debts and got in with the wrong kind of people. It didn't help that my grandfather raised him on the family folklore of William Shafer sitting on a stash of coins from working the Klondike Gold Rush. I think he believed William had cheated Henry out of his share."

Penny interrupted. "Papa, you cleared that up for us. We knew Henry had married William's girlfriend. What we didn't know was that he'd demanded half the farm and got paid for it."

Mark had one more question for them.

"Why did you come here? If you knew your brother was hunting the treasure, why did you come?"

Carl's face tightened with anguish. "I was naive. I thought if Penny and I came, I could interrupt his plan. I thought if he did try to do something, I'd be able to stop him."

"You didn't know he'd threaten your life." Penny spoke up. "Prison changed him," she said more quietly.

Dorothy stood and broke the silence. "You've been through so much. It was kind of you to come today."

Papa chimed in. "Hard to have family turn on you like that."

"Well, I can tell you, Carl, *this* family will have your back," Brett said.

"Does this mean Macie can sleep over again?" Caroline asked.

"Maybe. How about we eat the lunch Dorothy prepared?" Angela suggested. They relocated to the dining room, leaving the tension behind, the clatter of dishes and drinks mixing with light conversation. Soon the girls were asking if they could play, but Penny said they needed to leave soon.

"Oh, we almost forgot," Carl said. "We brought you this."

All eyes followed him to the sofa, where he picked up a shallow, square gift box. He handed it to Mark. "This belongs to you."

Mark took it and nodded. He set it under the tree, but Carl and Penny spoke in unison.

"Open it."

Mark looked around the room at all the expectant eyes. He untied the bow and lifted the lid.

He held up the quilted star tree topper so all could see.

How could it be?

Angela gasped. Dorothy exclaimed it was beautiful.

"That's the one my grandma bought at Goodwill," Caroline exclaimed.

"Where did you get this?" Mark asked Carl. "You said you weren't the buyer."

"I wasn't. My brother was. He and his girlfriend. She's done time for identity theft. Somehow they fooled the auction house and pulled it off."

"But how did you get it from him?" Angela asked, still in disbelief.

"That's the ironic part. He handed it over to me, said it was worthless. He said there's no map inside whatsoever."

"I stitched up the side he cut open," Penny said. "I hope I didn't make it worse."

Mark and Angela inspected the stitching. Turning it over, they saw the gold thread and instantly looked at each other.

"What? What is it?" Penny asked.

"The map isn't *inside* the star. The map *is* the star. Or the star is the map. Either way, this is it," Mark announced.

Everyone crowded around the star to see what Mark was talking about, but he handed it to Angela and frantically pulled all the neatly arranged gifts off the tree skirt.

Caroline "rescued" the presents Mark was tossing aside, presents she'd spent time lovingly arranging. Angela handed the star to Dorothy in order to help Mark. Macie cornered her parents, asking to sleep over, and Papa retreated to the dining room, moving the candle and pine-cone centerpiece out of the way.

"Here, Mark. Bring it here," he said.

They flipped the tree skirt over and spread it out on the table. Dorothy handed the star back to Angela, and everyone watched as she placed it in the center. She rotated it once, then twice, realizing that the shape and size of the points, though similar, had slight differences. The star could only fit the center of the tree skirt in one way. As it rested in the intended position, the room grew quiet, with all eyes fixed on what was now a complete map of their land.

"Gorgeous," Dorothy whispered.

"So much detail," Angela said.

"Do you see what I see?" Mark asked.

"Is that the south lot there?" Carl questioned.

"Here's the cabin, the farmhouse, and the barn," Mark continued.

"But what about the treasure?" Caroline asked.

"Don't suppose she thought to put a nice '*x* marks the spot' for us," Papa said.

Mark ran his hands lightly over the star. Beside him, Angela touched the gold stitches. There weren't many. She pointed to one spot.

"Actually," she said. "She might have done just that."

Dorothy leaned closer. "I think you're right. It's a very small . . ."

"X," their voices said together.

❋

They quickly narrowed down the location based on all the other structures.

"It couldn't be, could it?" Mark asked out loud as he looked at Carl. "We still have your brother's air compressor and ground blanket. Do you want to help me?"

"Now?" Angela, Penny, and Papa all asked at the same time.

Mark looked at all their faces. "This is it. That treasure is either right where this map says it is, or it never existed in the first place. I'm not waiting another day—another hour—until we find out which it is!"

❋

The map led them directly to the toolshed—the eight-by-eight-foot unassuming structure that had been used to store vegetables but had become the resting place for broken or outdated tools. The place where Mark's dad had hidden the box he'd found. The same place Mark had suspected and single-handedly tunneled out a wall—and found nothing.

With the *x* on the star placed squarely over the old root cellar, there was no more guessing and no more wasting time on the wall. They assembled the ground warmer equipment but hardly had the patience for it to work. They began digging two at a time. Mark was unwilling to take a break, leaving Carl to spell Papa.

❋

Angela stood outside with her arm linked through Dorothy's. Penny was walking at the edge of the trees with her sons, holding their hands in each of hers. Caroline and Macie were deep in conversation, walking in wide circles around them. The sun was getting low, and Angela suddenly remembered Christmas Day three years ago. She stood in this same spot, wondering about Mark and his farm and a treasure.

She heard her name, her mother's voice.

Oh, that's right! Mother!

She and Gary were coming for dinner, but the dinner wasn't ready because no one was in the farmhouse cooking it.

"Angela, is that you?"

Dorothy spotted her. "Heavens, is it that late already? We've done it now, haven't we?"

"It's not exactly our fault," Angela defended.

"I better get the roast in the oven or else we'll be eating at midnight."

"I don't know if we'll be able to pull the guys away from their shovels," Angela said.

"No one answered the door," her mother called as she approached.

"Still, I better get the food together. Look at you. It's freezing. Maybe you should come back inside with me."

"What, and miss all the excitement?" Angela joked.

"What excitement?" Cathy asked now that she and Gary had reached them. "When no one came to the door, I'd thought maybe you were at the hospital again."

"Three weeks, Mom. I still have three more weeks."

Dorothy was retreating, and Angela felt torn between going inside to help her and staying to find out what was under the toolshed. Either way, she had some explaining to do.

Penny offered to help Dorothy, claiming she couldn't stand the cold one more minute and the boys needed a bathroom break.

Cathy and Greg listened as Angela told them about Carl and the tree topper and the map and gold stitches.

"That star did have a map on it?" Cathy asked.

"Yes. It could only be understood when it was aligned with the tree skirt, so here we are."

They looked to the entrance of the toolshed, where Carl emerged, wiping his forehead.

He turned off the air compressor. "Plenty warm in there now," he said to no one in particular.

It was almost dark, and Cathy implored Angela to come inside with her. "Gary can stay here and call us if there's anything to see. Won't you, Gary?" she asked.

"Yes, go. Angela put your feet up," he said.

They walked away toward the farmhouse. Cathy asked when dinner would be ready. Angela was about to answer when they heard Mark shouting. They turned to see him emerging from the toolshed with a shovel in one hand and lifting something else in the other.

"Angela! It's gold!"

She ran before she knew she was running. Mark opened his fist, and gold coins fell from it. They looked back and forth to the gold then to each other.

"Come see the rest of it," he said.

She stepped into the cellar far enough to see the hole they'd dug, a mound of dirt up against the far side of the room. Carl was down in the hole. It had to be at least six feet deep, but there was a wooden crate at the bottom, or what was probably the remains of several crates. And what hadn't decayed. Gold coins.

So many coins, Angela felt light-headed trying to guess how many.

Mark escorted her back out. "It's stuffy in there. Get some fresh air."

All she could do was hug him. "I can't believe it, Mark, I really can't."

"I know," he said. "All this time, right under our feet!"

Angela was euphoric, bewildered, ecstatic—and cold. Even her often overheated pregnant body was no match for the freezing temperatures.

"You better get inside," Mark said when he saw her shiver.

"I think you're right," she said.

He hugged her one more time.

"Ow," she said and laughed. "That was a strong hug."

Mark quickly released her. "Sorry, you okay? It's the adrenaline. Sorry."

"I'm fine. Going now."

But as she turned to go, she felt a pop, then a warm rush.

"Mark!"

CHAPTER 25

The hospital had a skeleton crew, but that didn't stop Angela from having a crowd of nurses and assistants surrounding her in the maternity department. One nurse had the nerve to doubt Angela's water had broken, but that was confirmed soon enough. There was no denying the contractions she was having.

Mark had asked for Brett's help, and he gladly came back to the farm. Mark didn't even know what needed to be done but felt like he shouldn't leave the toolshed unattended. Carl and Penny had to get back to her sister's family. They vowed to keep the gold a secret.

Cathy and Gary said they would stay with Caroline and bring her to the hospital when Mark called.

All Angela could do was grab Mark's hand.

"I thought I had three more weeks, Mark. I thought I had three more weeks," she repeated.

"There was too much excitement. I'm sorry I got so caught up. You were standing outside too long after all that walking. I should have known better."

Angela stared at him for a minute.

"What? What's wrong?" he asked.

She burst out laughing.

Mark looked at the nurses with a slightly frightened expression. "Is she okay?"

"Mark, it's not your fault. I had to go into labor at some point. It's not every day you discover buried treasure."

Angela's voice was at a high pitch on the words *buried* and *treasure*. That surely got the nurses' attention. Angela looked nervously at Mark. He leaned in close, his forehead next to hers.

"I love you, Angela Shafer. I love you so much I can hardly breathe."

"I love you too. I'll focus on the breathing. How's that?" she said.

Unaffected by any conversation Mark and Angela were having, the nurses continued to come and check the monitors at sporadic intervals.

"You know, we were finally going to have our romantic anniversary celebration," Mark said.

"Yeah, about that." She exhaled sharply.

"If you had wanted to get out of it, you could have said something. You didn't have to go into labor!" Mark said.

"Believe me, this wasn't my idea."

Mark assessed their room. "There still might be time. I could find a palm tree and a few pineapples."

Angela laughed.

"I love that sound," he said as he squeezed her hand.

"Hey, guess what," she said through some deep breaths. "I know what I said before about making sure our anniversary didn't get lost in the holiday craziness, but that was before I knew what kind of husband you'd be."

"What kind is that?" he asked.

"The kind who loves me every day, not just once a year," she said.

"Are you saying you don't need a romantic date?"

"You being here, with me and for me—that's romantic."

❄

Five hours later, Joshua Shafer was born—all eight pounds, two ounces of him.

Angela didn't worry that it was December instead of January. She was too relieved and exhausted to care about anything besides her precious newborn son. She didn't know when her mother had arrived with Caroline, but there they were. Mark motioned for them to come in. He held Joshua, showing him off. Caroline hugged her mom and then peered at her new baby brother.

"He's pretty squishy, but he's got your eyebrows, Mom, and Mark's chin," she said.

"He's beautiful. A darling son you have," Cathy said as she reached for Angela's hand and looked at her with tears in her eyes.

Angela had never seen her mother so overcome with emotion or so genuinely, softheartedly happy.

"Thank you for being here, Mom. It means a lot."

"To me too," she said.

Angela looked up to see Mark at the door of their room greeting Papa and Dorothy. As they filed in, Cathy and Caroline left. The hugs and congratulations flowed freely, as did the tears. Angela loved watching Papa stare at his great-grandson with so much love in his eyes like Joshua was a treasure. Yes, that was it—*he* was the real treasure. Then Angela noticed Mark standing beside her. He was looking at her with that same mix of love and wonder. Her tears came without effort.

"What day is it, Mark?" she asked.

His eyes widened. "Is it…"

"Merry Christmas!" she said. "To us and our newest Christmas miracle."

ACKNOWLEDGMENTS

Thank you first, to all the readers who have followed Mark and Angela on their journey. Your loyalty and support spurred me to continue their story.

My sincerest thanks go to Michele Preisendorf of Eschler Editing, whose skillful editing provided needed polish and shine.

Thank you to Sweetly Us Book Services for the lovely cover and E. A. Smart III for the inspired illustration.

I offer heartfelt thanks to Valerie, Peggy, and Anika, my allies in the whirlwind, for their invaluable encouragement. And to countless members of ANWA and my writing group, for vital feedback and friendship.

I could dedicate all the words I write to my mother, my first and most dedicated fan. Without her love, support, and encouragement to live my best life, I couldn't have written this book or any others. A simple thank-you doesn't seem adequate, but in her words, "I love you is always enough." So, mom, thank you for everything. And I love you.

Writing may be solitary work, but I couldn't do it without my family cheering me on. Thank you to my children for their love and hugs. Finally, my deepest gratitude goes to my husband. Thank you, Steve, for making it clear who and what you treasure.

ABOUT THE AUTHOR

Tamara Passey, author of the #1 Amazon bestseller, *The Christmas Tree Keeper: A Novel*, loves crafting a story. She was born and raised in Massachusetts surrounded by a large family, one that has served as inspiration for much of her writing. She loves most creative endeavors, and when she isn't writing, you can find her reading, baking, or hiking in the desert. She lives with her husband and children in Arizona.

Visit Tamara and sign up for her newsletter online at www.tamarapassey.com.

Made in the USA
Columbia, SC
17 November 2024